MAIN STREET
Home for Christmas

Other **MAIN STREET** *Books by*
Susan E. Kirby

MAIN STREET: LEMONADE DAYS

Coming Soon

MAIN STREET: HOME FRONT HERO

"Take the hard road," are familiar words to author SUSAN E. KIRBY, who has lived most of her life with Route 66 at her doorstep. But never was the phrase more fitting to America's Main Street than during the Great Depression. HOME FOR CHRISTMAS is a tribute to Susan's maternal grandparents whose faith, love and courage triumphed over hard times and hard knocks during Oklahoma's dust bowl days.

MAIN STREET
Home for Christmas

SUSAN E. KIRBY

AN AVON CAMELOT BOOK

MAIN STREET: HOME FOR CHRISTMAS is an original publication of Avon
Books. This work has never before appeared in book form. Any similarity to actual
persons or events is purely coincidental.

AVON BOOKS
A division of
The Hearst Corporation
1350 Avenue of the Americas
New York, New York 10019

Copyright © 1994 by Susan E. Kirby
Published by arrangement with the author
Library of Congress Catalog Card Number: 94-94460
ISBN: 0-380-77407-0
RL: 4.6

First Avon Camelot Printing: October 1994

CAMELOT TRADEMARK REG. U.S. PAT OFF. AND IN OTHER COUNTRIES, MARCA REGISTRADA,
HECHO EN U.S.A.

Printed in the U.S.A.

OPM 10 9 8 7 6 5 4 3 2 1

For my mother, Glaida Funk
In memory of my grandparents Earl and Ethel Wade

ACKNOWLEDGMENTS

Thank you, Elizabeth Harkins, for sharing your memories of how a little girl, a thorn tree, and a surprise party brought home the true meaning of Christmas in the midst of hard times.

One

---◆◆◆---

Clement, Oklahoma
1932

The pop crate creaked beneath Suker Tucker's feet as she stood counting the cash drawer at the Flying Red Horse. Seven dollars and ten cents. Just like the first two times. She liked to handle the money. But she'd been at the gas station since school let out, and her belly was growling.

The door between the small station and the mechanic garage was standing open. She trotted over the threshold. "Dave? Can we go home now?"

Her foster father, Dave Tilton, paused in adjusting the plugs on a Model T. He moved the lantern just so, then turned to ask, "You hungry?"

Suker nodded.

Dave wiped his hands on a rag and beckoned toward the highway. "Walk on out to the road and see what's comin'."

Other merchants in Clement kept regular hours. Not Dave. He'd stay at the garage until the traffic stopped. Even later, when he was working beneath the hood of an auto. Suker pulled a long face in the wide window glass.

Oklahoma topsoil blurred her blue-eyed, freckle-faced reflection. The wind, out of the east, had left an orange film on her skin, her feed-sack dress, and her wispy hair. She pushed her arms into Maggie's hand-me-down coat, then paused to turn Dave's calendar page to December.

"Be Christmas before you know it."

"So it will," said Dave, in that careful way of his.

Suker broke into a pigeon-toed amble, crossing the hard-packed drive to the edge of Highway 66. Dave kept real busy at the garage. Trouble was, a lot of folks paid in vouchers and promises. Some passing through just couldn't pay at all. Dave'd give them enough gas to get them to the next station down the road, where they'd do the same. It was the sensible thing, keeping travelers from getting stranded where there was no work. But it sure kept Dave strapped for cash, so strapped Sophie'd said there'd be no fuss this Christmas.

But what was Christmas without fuss? Separation, that's what. Suker stood in the night, thinking of Christmases past. Of her brother, Razz, and her father and their snug little house in the lush green woods just north of Shirley. Pungent pine needles, savory venison, and tangy oranges scented the memories. Mouth watering, Suker thought too of nuts and sweets and baby-doll Clarisse, her last gift from her father. A hurting swept over her, so sharp she caught her breath.

"Anything coming?" called Dave from the doorway of the station.

The Flying Red Horse was the last stop on the west end of Clement. Beyond the garage, the dusty highway melted across the plains, blending into the dark lavender horizon. Back toward the streetlights of Clement, it was

2

just as empty. Suker poked her hands into her pockets and called, "Not a car in sight."

But just as Dave pulled the Closed sign onto the drive, Suker saw a pair of headlights turn onto the highway from one of Clement's side streets.

"Wait up," she called.

The twin lights came winking down the road. It was the rural mail carrier, Harvey Markham. He was a heavyset, worrisome fellow. He fussed and fumed and smiled so rarely he'd earned himself the nickname "Happy." He climbed out of his car and gave Dave a droopy nod.

"Ten gallons. I'll have to sign for it. I'm flyin' Hoover flags till payday."

"Hoover flags," Suker knew, meant empty pockets. President Hoover'd be leaving the White House soon, since Mr. Roosevelt had won the recent election. But for the time being, at least, folks were laying the nation's poverty at his doorstep.

There was a glass globe on top of the hand-operated pump. As Dave pumped, the gasoline passed through the globe down into the glass cylinder. Once it filled to the ten-gallon level, he aimed the nozzle into the tank of the mail carrier's car.

Happy scratched a sagging jaw. "Harrisons cleared out in the night. Just ahead of the sheriff and eviction papers."

"So I heard," said Dave.

"Tractored out. Just like the others." Happy spat in the dry plains dirt. "What's a fella to do?"

"Dunno." Dave kept his eye on the cylinder.

"They was headed west. Thought there'd be peas or lettuce or somethin' to pick in California."

"Hope it works out for 'em," said Dave.

"Course, it don't hit you like it does some. Folks givin' up, headin' west got to have gas. Cars break down, they got to be fixed."

Suker didn't think Happy ought to make out like Dave was profiting from the bad fortune of others. She poked out her chin. "Isn't Dave's fault. He didn't turn them out."

Happy's bushy brows drew together. He clutched his hand-rolled cigarette between stubby fingers and motioned to Suker. "Scrap of a thing like you, don't know nothin' about nothin'."

Indignation stiffened Suker's spine, for she did so know. But a look from Dave was warning enough. She walked away rather than shame him by back-talking her elders. A tumbleweed got in her way. She gave it a kick. Out-of-work hard timers hung around the Flying Red Horse, teaching her plenty just by their idle talk.

Then there was her teacher, Miss Cadlow. And the testimony of empty seats. There'd been eighteen students in Suker's class at the beginning of the school term. Now there were twelve. Some of those missing were the children of tenant farmers, moved off the land by drought, by default on loans, and by landlords replacing them with tractors. Others were the children of merchants who'd closed their doors and moved on.

As soon as Happy signed for his gas and went on his way, Dave locked up for the night. They started home along Highway 66, Clement's main street, heading east. Head east long enough, seven hundred-odd miles and a body'd be in Shirley. Suker was pleased knowing that, for it made separation nothing more than a very long walk.

A coal train rumbled along on the other side of the highway. It creaked and groaned beneath its cumbersome load. Sometimes, when things were slow at the garage, Suker walked the tracks, picking up coal that'd spilled off. "Pennies saved," as Sophie always said, "is pennies earned."

Dave said, as they passed the post office, "There's nothing to gain by butting heads with fellas like Happy."

"He's got no call to be sore at you."

"Can't take it personal. He's sore at the world."

"Don't know why. He's got a job, ain't he?" said Suker. Her stomach was howling in earnest now.

"Yes, but some of his neighbors don't. And a couple of his boys have been tractored out. He's hurting for them," Dave explained.

"Still, it's not *your* fault."

Dave's big work-rough hand closed over hers. " 'preciate your loyalty, Suker. But in all fairness, there's some truth to what Happy says. Folks are as worn-out and footloose as the soil. And if they're following a dream in a motor car, then it takes fuel and spare parts and tires and a heap of other things we stock."

Back in Illinois, Suker's daddy'd done time for moonshining. It was a bitter pill—to be shunned, to be pitied, to be shamed. She turned her face up, feeling anxious. "Don't mean we ought to be ashamed, does it?"

"Course not. We're providing a service." Dave squeezed her hand. "I like to think we're helping folks down on their luck find a better life."

A car rolled passed, plip-plipping over the lonely pavement. There was a mattress roped to the top. A goat

5

and some chickens were crated to the sideboard. More dreamers following the hard road west.

Suker looked back toward the Flying Red Horse. "Reckon they'd of stopped if you'd been there?"

Dave said, without looking back, "Don't hurt to leave a few for the next fella down the pike."

Streetlamps spilled puddles of light along Clement's business district. Solid brick buildings on both sides of the street gave the little town a prosperous look. But up close, it was a different story. A going-out-of-business sign hung off center in the window of Midge's Wee Needle. The dance hall was vacant, and a hat shop too. Some of the buildings, which were empty even before they'd settled in Clement last spring, had paint-bare trim and broken glass and debris strewn about.

Suker noticed a light burning in Blossom's General Merchandise. Roly-poly Mr. Blossom was trimming his window with tinsel. The silvery strands struck sparks off Suker. She freed her hand from Dave's. "At least *some* folks are planning on Christmas coming as usual."

"Can't keep it from coming, Suker. Wouldn't if I could." Dave shoved his hands in his pockets and kept walking.

Hurrying to catch up, Suker stole a quick glance at his profile. He seemed earnest enough. "Sophie says there'll be no fuss. You said it too," she reminded.

"Won't be," Dave maintained. "But Christmas ain't about fuss, anyway. It's about God's baby boy coming and a world with no room. You know that."

Suker felt as if he'd turned the tables on her. Grown-ups, even soft-spoken ones like Dave, could turn words to their own advantage.

Yet wasn't saying there'd be no fuss the same as say-

6

ing there was no room? Suker pondered it some as they turned down a quiet dirt street. Clement was a rural town. The only folks with electricity were those who could afford Delco generators. But oil lanterns and candles made a soft glow from windows here and there.

Their house was at the end of the street. Anticipating a hot meal, a warm fire, and Maggie and Sophie waiting, Suker quickened her step.

But Dave paused at Miss Greer Tims's gate. There was a meager light burning inside. "I'll wait right here. Check, see," he said.

Dutifully, Suker let herself through the gate. She wished daily that she hadn't knocked over her elderly neighbor's birdbath last June. Had she known it'd doom her to a lifetime of check-sees, she never would have struck back at Miss Tims for tattling on her over the cherries she'd swiped from the old stick's tree.

"Louder," said Dave from the gate.

Suker knocked again and the light drew closer. Miss Tims opened the door a crack. She was a tall woman, thin and knobby as a post. The only spare flesh was a loose wattle just below her chin. Her dark eyes narrowed upon Suker's face.

"You're late, Susan," she said.

"Yes, ma'am. We was working," murmured Suker.

"You *were* working." Miss Tim pinched up her nose as if bad grammar had a stench to it.

"Yes, ma'am, we sure were. Can—" Suker pinched back a stubborn streak and corrected herself, saying, "May I empty your ashes or carry some coal?"

"That won't be necessary tonight. But perhaps you could stop by in the morning."

"Yes, ma'am. I will."

7

"Good night, Susan."

"Night." Relieved at getting off so easy, Suker took the steps fast and muttered to Dave, "Hurry, b'fore she changes her mind."

Instead of hurrying, he tipped his hat and said, "Evening, Miss Tims."

Miss Tims nodded and closed the door quick. Folks said she didn't like men nor boys either, not even little ones. Course, they also said she wandered the cemetery at night, swearing at her brothers, dead and buried. And according to the post office gossips, the bones of a man who'd come courting were bleaching white in her basement.

Suker knew better. She'd fetched canned goods from the basement plenty of times for Miss Tims. Still, just having heard it said gave her the chills every time she started down those dank, dingy steps.

"Ought never to have told her my birth name," groused Suker as she and Dave mounted their own sagging porch steps.

"She's from the old school where a name means something," said Dave.

A name *did* mean something, when there was love behind it. Her mama, who'd died before Suker was old enough to remember, had given her the name Susan. But Pa had called her Suker and her brother, Raymond Azariah, he'd nicknamed Razz. Miss Foster, the schoolteacher back in Shirley who'd taken her in while her father had served out his nine-month prison term, called her Suker. Sophie and Maggie and Dave went along with it, too. Suker, that's who she was.

Miss Greer Tims had a different idea. She thought a body was dutybound to live up to her given name. "Susan," she'd told Suker, came from the Hebrew name, Susannah, meaning "lily," and that she ought to work a good deal harder at being as pure and lovely as a lily.

"Greer," then, must mean "keen-eyed and critical," for nothing moved along their street that Miss Greer Tims didn't see and criticize. Suker'd become acquainted with *that* truth the hard way!

TWO

The house they'd rented upon settling in Clement was roomy enough. But time and neglect had taken their toll. The floors were uneven, the walls patched and water stained. There was no keeping up with the dust sifting through doors and window sashes. And at night, when the lanterns were lit, shadows danced in the draft.

But it was shelter and warmth and supper cooking. Suker's heart lifted as she followed Dave in. She glanced past the potbellied stove to Sophie's homemade quilt frame with a quilt in progress. Yes sir, a Christmas tree'd fit there just fine.

Maggie came grinning through the dining room. She was short and slight for seventeen. A wave of dark hair framed a comely face. Her hazel eyes twinkled with fun as she kept one hand hidden in her apron pocket. "Guess what I have here, Suker. Something for you."

The stamp peeked over the edge of her pocket. Suker caught her breath. "From Razz?" she asked, hushed-like.

Maggie bobbed her head and passed it over. Suker let

out a glad cry. She shrugged out of her coat and raced to the kitchen, hugging the letter tight.

"A letter, Sophie! Look!"

"Yes sir, that's what I hear." Sophie turned from the stove. A forelock of hair fell across her brow. "There's a knife, there on the table."

Suker slid it under the flap. Five months. Five long months since she'd had a letter from Razz. And now, a nice thick one! She leaned against the table where the lantern shone brightest. Razz had, upon their father's death, been left in the care of the preacher. He'd been a stickler about Razz doing his schoolwork and, these days, Razz wrote a pretty fair hand. His tone came right through as sure as if he were standing there.

Dear Sis,

Hunting's fair. I got my traps oiled, just waiting for snow. Get a day's work in now and agin. But a steady job's hard to come by. I been courtin' Kitty Maxwell. Reckon you remember her. Prettier than ever. Her ma doesn't like me much. Says I'm just like Pa. Says it right to my face. I hold my head up and grin like it pleases me. You remember that, Suker. Don't let folks beat you down.

How's Maggie? Remember when she sat on a tack and jumped up so quick, I spilled ink on her dress and she told Miss Foster the tack was mine? She didn't know it, but I was sweet on her then. Makes me laugh now to think how spunky she was. I reckon you're all right with Maggie for a sister. She always was partial to you. I know it was her talked her mama into taking you in when Pa

11

was killed. Reckon if Sophie hadn't married Dave Tilton you'd be living here in Shirley still. But then, how were we to know Dave'd follow the highway out, paving Oklahoma 66?

Say, you remember Mr. Jeremiah Bishop? Well, he shot himself last week. Folks say he'd been down in the dumps over losing his farm and his money and the bank threatening eviction. Guess losing his wife to the flu epidemic was just the last straw. Folks around here are clacking their tongues, layin' bets as to whether Bryce is man enough to raise his little brother. I say he isn't. But then, it always did stick in my craw he wasn't charged with bootlegging right along with Pa. Pa was right, you know. It's who you are, not what you done, that counts where the law's concerned.

Was hunting wild turkey last week when I came across a piece of twisted copper. Must have been half a mile from where Pa's still blew. Gave me the shivers all over again to think of him going that way. Made me lonesome for the days when we lived in the woods. Right then, I decided to come see how much growing you've done in the four years since you left Shirley. I've got no money for train fare. But I'm coming somehow. Hope to make it by Christmas, so you be smoothing the way with Sophie and Dave, you hear? See you soon.

YOUR BROTHER, RAZZ

Suker let out a yell and flung herself at Sophie. "He's coming, Sophie! He's coming!"

"Razz? Coming here?" Sophie's voice echoed surprise. But then she didn't know just how hard Suker'd been praying.

Maggie grinned, sharing Suker's moment. "That's wonderful, Suker. Would you wash up now? I'm starved."

Suker wiggled out of Sophie's arms and beamed at Dave, full of joy. Her brother was coming. Nothing could stop Christmas now!

Razz-a-razz-a, the creaky pump squeaked with each downward stroke. Suker stuck her face under the pump and gurgled jubilantly as Dave worked the black handle. He laughed and so did Maggie. Sophie draped a feed-sack towel across Suker's shoulder.

"Yer splashing," she said. But there was a smile in her voice.

The enamel basin sitting in the sink had caught the runoff from Suker's washing. Dave splashed his face and hands in the same basin, then set it to one side. Maggie carried it over to the stove to be reused later for puddling out a few clothes.

Suker slipped into her chair. The navy bean soup smelled like heaven. They'd had it yesterday, too, only with corn bread on the side. Tonight, there were dumplings floating on top. Cold hard-boiled eggs and peaches looked mighty good too. The peaches were a special treat, as Sophie's larder of home-canned goods was growing sparse. A good bit of last summer's garden had withered and died, what with the drought.

Dave bowed his head. His voice rumbled deep in the warmth of the spacious kitchen. "Dear Heavenly Father, bless this food to the nourishment of our bodies. And bless the hands that prepared it. Amen."

"Amen," Suker echoed.

Sophie dished up the soup. A hot ember sizzled in the big black range as cutlery clinked against dishes. Suker closed her eyes, savoring the warmth of food filling her belly. A couple more bites, and she confided, "Razz thinks he'll be here in time for Christmas."

"Winter's a tricky time to travel," said Dave.

Misunderstanding the cautious glance he exchanged with Sophie, Suker's pulse quickened. "He won't eat much, Dave. And if he does, well, I'll just eat less."

"You're nothing but skin and bones now," said Maggie.

Sensitive about being a runt, Suker retorted, "Ain't 'cause I don't eat. I eat a lot."

"Sure you do. You've got a good appetite," said Maggie, quick to cover her error.

"I can do with less, though."

"No call for that. We'll be glad to have Razz visit a spell," Dave soothed.

"Razz can have my bed. I'll sleep with Maggie. Or maybe he'd rather have the attic room. Guess what? Razz says he's been courting Kitty Maxwell," Suker rattled on.

"Kitty Maxwell!" Maggie grinned wickedly. "Dainty as a doily, dull as a dipstick."

"Maggie," said Sophie, tone disapproving.

Maggie tossed her dark head and laughed. "I'll never forget the time I said Kitty's poem for Miss Foster's class. It was Kitty's fault as much as mine. She'd said it all the way to school, over and over again. I was nervous as could be when it came my turn. Lo and behold, out popped Kitty's poem. Remember, Suker? You were there. I could *still* say it word for word."

14

Suker didn't remember. But she laughed to think of it. "Let's hear."

Maggie rose from her chair and said with great drama: "The Hired Man's Faith in Children, by James Whitcomb Riley. 'I believe *all* children's good, if they're only *understood,* Even *bad* ones 'pears to me, Is jest as good as they kin be!' "

Dave stroked his upper lip, thoughtful-like. "I might take issue with that. There's a certain Rob Kelsey fella been comin' around, I'm not too sure about. What do you think, Suker?"

Suker took her cue from his wink. "No better'n a common thief. A 'Pretty Boy' Floyd, robbing kisses instead of banks."

Maggie's cheeks glowed pink, but her eyes danced with laughter. "Just listen to them, Mama!"

"I'm listenin'. And what I'm hearin' is that they like this Rob Kelsey fella well enough." Sophie's smile glowed soft, binding them close.

Rob was okay. Just so long as he didn't move Maggie west like so many rural folks were doing. Not wanting to dwell on that, Suker turned her thoughts back to Razz's letter. All at once, she realized she'd left out a real juicy piece of news.

"You know that Mr. Bishop you used to work for, Sophie? The one whose wife died not long ago? Well, seems he'd been sad over losing his farm and his money and everything. So he up and shot himself."

"Jeremiah Bishop?" Maggie dropped her fork.

All the pleasure drained from Sophie's face, and the color with it. "You're saying he's dead? Suker, are you sure?"

Suker nodded. Her gaze skipped from Sophie's face

to Maggie's and on to Dave's. She squirmed in her chair. She ought to have broken the news more gently.

Sophie said, "Could I see the letter, Suker? Just the part about Mr. Bishop?"

Reluctantly, Suker turned her treasure over. She needn't have worried about Sophie reading the parts she didn't want her to see. One quick glance and she passed it back, saying in a tight, worried voice, "First Polly, now his daddy! Razz is right, you know. Bryce'll never look after the little one. Dear Lord, what'll become of the poor child?"

"Could be yer not giving Bryce enough credit," Dave murmured. "He could have grown up a heap in four years."

Maggie jabbed at a dumpling. "Not to hear Clara tell it, he hasn't. In her last letter, she mentioned Bryce. Said he's still the talk of Shirley, cars and young ladies still take up most of his time."

Sophie rubbed at a stain on the tabletop. "Bryce is like a child himself. He just never has taken on any responsibility."

Sophie wasn't one for fretting and stewing and giving into tears. But Suker could tell, as the dishes were emptied, washed, and put away, that the news had really shaken her. Was it Mr. Bishop's death causing the upset? Or the child he'd left behind? The boy she and Maggie had always called the little one.

Suker wished she'd kept Mr. Bishop's suicide to herself. It sure put a damper on the evening. After a while, she shut out their talk and started planning Christmas in her head. She saw the tree, festive with homemade decorations. Some sweets would be nice too. Maggie, who hadn't been able to find work since graduating from high school, baked bread and sold it at the station to travelers passing through. Maybe she'd make a special Christmas bread. Or a red velvet cake. Wouldn't that be fine! Once Dave retired to the front room, Suker washed herself good and changed into her nightgown. She rinsed out her clothes in the basin of water and hung them by the stove to dry. Then she went upstairs, for Maggie, then Sophie and Dave would follow the same procedure.

Her room was right over the kitchen, with an iron grate in the floor to let up some heat. But in cold weather, it wasn't enough to make the room comfortable. Suker crawled beneath a layer of quilts and warmed her a toasty spot, thinking about Razz and Christmas and tingling with goodwill.

After a bit, Suker heard Dave go off to bed. Slipping into her shoes, she crept back down to the kitchen. Sophie was unbraiding her hair by the stove. It hung halfway to her waist, a nice chestnut brown with some gray running through. Static cracked and popped as she set in brushing. Suker counted strokes.

"I'm sorry about Mr. Bishop being dead and all," she said when Sophie'd reached one hundred strokes. "And I know you said no fuss. But just seems to me like we ought to have a tree for Christmas, what with Razz coming and all."

Sophie's hairbrush drifted to her lap. Her gray gaze searched Suker's face. After a moment, she gave up the chair, saying, "Sit."

Suker sat, letting Sophie run the brush through her hair. She closed her eyes, enjoying the way the bristles made her scalp tingle.

"Razz means to come, I'm sure." Sophie measured

her words with each brush stroke. "But don't get yer hopes up too much. Winter's set on, and to be real honest, Suker, I just don't know how he'll manage to get here."

It was like a hot knife to tender flesh. Suker jerked out of the chair. "He'll come, Sophie. He promised!"

Sophie was quiet a moment. "All right, then. Just so you understand."

Resenting the pitying look on Sophie's face, Suker dashed up the back stairs to her own little room. She crawled into bed, hugging her doll, Clarisse. He would *too* come. He would.

She heard Dave's footsteps descending the stairs, then his voice in the kitchen below. His words were too soft to carry up through the grate. But by lying real quiet, she heard enough to know it was the little one occupying Sophie's thoughts.

"God love him, I just can't bear to think how he must be hurting right now. And scared! Wouldn't you, if Bryce Bishop was all that stood between you and an orphanage?"

Dave's voice rumbled low, and Sophie came back again, saying, "Polly's family, out on the east coast. But I don't think they'll take him. They never approved the marriage, Mr. Bishop bein' so much older than Polly. Polly's sister came for a visit once, but it didn't go well. She went home in a huff, and Polly never heard a word after that. And her not being well herself. I cared for the little fellow like he was my own. Reckon that's why it cuts so deep."

It was unsettling, Sophie so sorry sounding. Suker covered her ears, not wanting to hear any more. Gradually the voices stopped and the house grew quiet around her.

But the weight on her chest grew heavier and heavier until it was hard to breathe past the fear. It was no ordinary fear, like fear of the dark or bodies in Miss Greer Tims's basement or thieves like "Pretty Boy" Floyd coming through town on a robbing spree. No, it was fear of coming awake to find herself completely alone.

Taking Clarisse with her, Suker crept across the hall to Maggie's room. Crawling beneath the covers quietly, she eased her foot right up against Maggie's. Maggie jerked.

"Sorry," murmured Suker.

But she didn't move her foot. And Maggie didn't make her. Instead, she sandwiched it between her own warm ones and whispered, "Mama doesn't know everything, Suker. You just keep trusting he'll come, you hear?"

Three

———◦———

Back in Shirley, Illinois, a little boy stood in the window of a fine brick house. Across the snowy drive, his grown-up half-brother was loading a box into the black touring car.

The car had belonged to the boy's father. So had the house. And everything in it. But Father was gone. Mother, too. And a red-faced, shuffle-footed sheriff had come with a piece of paper that said they had to get out.

"Eviction." That was the word.

The boy's wool knickers itched. He was hungry, too, for Bryce had forgotten to fix lunch. But mostly he was concerned about leaving. How would Mother and Father find him, if they should come back? He asked Bryce when he came in.

His brother's hand trembled as it came to rest on Jeremiah's shoulder. "Look, chum, this stinks for both of us. But you've got to understand, they aren't coming back."

"But what if they do?"

"Believe me, they won't."

Worry had changed Bryce. He looked older and not so sure of himself. He *could* be mistaken. Jere worked a loose tooth with his tongue. "Why not?"

Bryce ran a hand through his thick, black hair. His eyes were dull. "Do you want to go see the graves?" he said finally. "We could stop by in the morning before we leave."

Jeremiah wagged his head. He hadn't liked it out there where the wind blew on rows of white stones. The preacher saying words over a yawning hole. Women he didn't even know crying and hugging him and saying they were sorry.

Bryce pulled a silver flask from a high shelf. He took a long drink, then came back, smelling like medicine. "Tell you what, chum. If it'll make you feel any better, leave a note. You've got your school tablet, don't you?"

Jeremiah found his tablet. He waited patiently while Bryce took another drink from the flask. "What shall I say?"

"Say we're going to California. Maybe we'll stop in Oklahoma to see Sophie and Maggie. I received a letter, inviting us." Bryce patted his shirt pocket.

Jeremiah had been to school only part of one year. The names were strange and hard to spell. He pushed the tablet into Bryce's hands. "Draw it."

"A map? All right."

Bryce drew a straight line across the page. He made three *x*'s along the line. "This is Highway 66. We're here in Shirley. This is Oklahoma, where Sophie lives. And this is California."

"Write it, please?"

Bryce labeled all three *x*'s. He returned the tablet to

Jere. "Write your note now, while I finish loading the car."

Jeremiah didn't know what to say. So he drew a picture of the car. He put a round face in the window and a hand waving. "Love," he wrote. Then he signed his name, all eight letters.

He studied it a moment, not quite satisfied. It didn't explain why. Eviction was why. Another hard word. Bryce would know how to spell it. He opened the door, intending to ask. But there was a grown-up boy out there talking to Bryce. He was shorter than Bryce and thin. His hair was brown and wiry and his face looked familiar. Jeremiah stared, trying to place him.

"There isn't room," said Bryce. "We're taking everything we can pack in."

The boy hunched his shoulders against the wind. His jacket was worn shiny thin. "If you won't do it for me, do it for my pa's sake."

Bryce crammed his hands in his pockets and looked away. "I appreciate your wanting to see your little sister. And I don't mean to seem hard toward the memory of your father. But I've got trials of my own."

"I won't be a burden, far from it." The boy stood his ground. "I'm handy with tools, should the car break down. And I can spell you with the driving."

Bryce turned up the flask, shaking out the last drops. He drew a hand across his mouth.

"If it's Dutch courage you're needing, I reckon I could find you some 'shine," the boy offered.

Bryce's face contorted. "They've foreclosed on the farm and kicked us out of the house. I've got two thousand miles of road ahead and a kid on my hands who doesn't understand the word 'dead'! If that wouldn't shake a fellow—"

"It's some Pa hid away. He made the best," the boy interrupted. "Not that I have to tell *you.*"

"Brazen little beggar, aren't you?" Bryce's temper flared.

The boy shrugged. "I drive real good. I'll even explain 'dead' to the little fellow. Why, we'll be regular pals by the time we reach Oklahoma. And, unless I miss my guess, he's going to need a familiar face right about then."

Bryce's gaze slid away from the boy's hard-jawed look. "You don't understand."

"I'm not passing judgment. All I want is a ride."

Suddenly, Jeremiah remembered where he'd seen the boy. In the cellar! He'd gone down there for strawberry preserves the last time Bryce had forgotten dinner. The boy had been sitting on a barrel, eating out of a jar. For one brief moment, they'd stared at each other. Then the boy had dashed out the cellar door, leaving behind a half-eaten jar of tomatoes.

Jeremiah had raced upstairs to tell Bryce. He'd found him in his mama's room with a lady friend. He'd blurted out the story. But Bryce had roughed his hair and smiled at the lady, saying, "Jere's our story boy. Clever, isn't he?"

It was then Jeremiah had realized Bryce was giving his mama's dresses away. He'd run out to the walnut grove. He had not meant to cry, for his father had frowned on boys crying. Finally, the cold drove him back to the house. Bryce explained that he had to give the dresses away. That when the sheriff came again, they'd lose whatever was left in the house. He said that his lady friend was just keeping the dresses safe.

Jeremiah wiggled his tooth with his tongue and looked at the tablet in his hand. He'd leave the note upstairs on Mother's dressing table. If she came back, she'd be sure to find it there.

A hairbrush and some bright glittery jewelry was all that remained in the dressing table. Jeremiah slipped the jewelry into the sock along with his life savings—six silver dollars. He didn't want his mother's hairbrush to fall into the hands of the sheriff. So he took it too. He walked out and closed the door. But he wasn't crying. It was just his eyes leaking a little.

The next morning, Jeremiah said good-bye to the house and climbed into the touring car. The boy was at the end of the lane, waiting. Bryce stopped, and he crowded in, bringing only a medicine bottle and a flour sack with a few belongings. The bottle, he passed to Bryce.

Jeremiah didn't speak to the boy the first day, nor the second day either. He had no use for a boy who ate food out of other folks' cellars. But the boy took up for him in a way that was hard not to notice.

"Pull over," he'd say, "Jere has to pee." Or, "Jere's hungry." Or once in Missouri, "Jere ought to see this here cave. They been advertising it for a hundred miles."

Bryce paid their way in, and they saw the cave where outlaws once hid out. Jeremiah didn't like it much; it was damp and dark and eerie. But he did like the picnics they had in the car. And the hills and bluffs just outside the car window. And the cabin where they spent the second night.

The third day, they had several flat tires. And twice, in eastern Oklahoma where the soil was bright as a red Crayola, they broke down. The boy used baling wire and a couple of wrenches to get the car running again.

They lost a lot of time that day and had gone no great distance when the sky turned a mean gray. The wind spit red soil till it was hard to see. They were between towns when darkness came. Bryce ran off the road on a curve and stuck them in loose soil up to the axles.

"We'll get her out in the morning," said the boy.

But Bryce thought he saw a light in the distance. If it was a farmhouse, there'd be a team to pull them out.

Jeremiah and the boy ate bread and jam while they waited for Bryce to return. The cold crept in. They stretched out on the front seat and huddled beneath a pile of blankets so heavy, the weight of them wore Jeremiah out. The wind yowled like a cat and shook the car in its fury. Jeremiah was afraid Bryce wasn't coming back. It was so cold, so dark and dusty. Like a hole in the ground. He started in coughing and ended up crying.

"If this ain't a fix," said the boy. "I could cry myself. Here, this should help with the dust some."

He gave Jeremiah a damp rag to put over his nose and mouth. It did help keep him from choking on dust. The boy wet a rag for himself. He told about having a pony that'd stop when he whistled. He told about living with a preacher until just recently when he finished high school and came of age. And he spoke of his father dying and his mama dying too.

Jeremiah broke his three-day silence. "Did they come back?"

"No, they didn't."

"Couldn't they get out of the ground?" He found words for his worst fear.

"That isn't them in the ground. That's just their skins. I touched my pa, just before they closed the lid on the box. It was like touching a melon, all hard and cool and waxy," said the boy matter-of-factly. "It was just his skin, don't you see."

Jeremiah remembered his mother's warmth and fragrance. Her skin was soft as a petal on a rose. He edged a little closer, chills tingling his spine. "Where did they go?"

"The preacher says there's a better place," said the boy. "He says we can't see it yet."

"But where?" Jeremiah persisted. "Where are they?"

The boy pat-patted him. "There, there, now. You quit your worrying. Why, I reckon they're knocking on Heaven's gate as we speak."

The boy talked on in words that painted pictures in Jeremiah's mind. Pictures of white-robed angels waiting. Of shining light and beautiful music. The pictures softened his grief and eased his worry some. By and by, he drifted to sleep. When he awoke, it was daylight. The wind had stopped blowing, and the boy was no longer beside him.

Jeremiah looked up to see a shovelful of red dirt fly past the dirty window. The boy was digging them out. He climbed out to watch and waded into oily dust up to his waist.

The boy just wagged his head and said, "What a piece of country."

After a bit, Jeremiah saw a wagon coming. His heart

lifted as it drew nearer. Bryce was there on the seat beside a wrinkled old farmer.

Once they were underway again, drifts of dust on the road made for slow going. They passed a car creeping along with a mattress strapped to the roof. It was crammed full of household belongings and children. As the day dragged on, Jeremiah saw more such cars.

They got lost in Oklahoma City. A muddy dirt road took them past shacks thrown together out of sheets of tin, crates, and rusted-out car bodies. A girl, no bigger than Jeremiah, was walking along carrying a bucket. She was wearing boy's shoes and socks for gloves. She jutted out a dirty chin and stared back at him.

" 'Hooverville,' " the boy read a cardboard sign. "Reckon folks really live here?"

"They lost their homes. Poor devils," said Bryce. He turned his eyes away, as if it hurt to look.

Jeremiah remembered that word "eviction." His stomach twisted. Frightened by thoughts he dared not put into words, he crawled into the backseat. He made a nest for himself between boxes. Worn out by worry and travel and sadness, he slept right up until dusk.

When he awoke, he lay still, noticing a difference in the country. It'd flattened out. The red soil had given way to gray. After a bit, he yawned and stretched and started back over the seat. All at once, he stopped short. The boy was gone! Alarmed, he looked at his brother.

"Where is he?"

"Who, Razz?" Bryce's smile was thin. "He got out last time I stopped for gas."

"What about his sister?" asked Jeremiah.

"Guess he changed his mind."

That seemed odd to Jeremiah. He wondered as he

27

reached beneath the seat if Bryce had quarreled with the boy or tired of his company. But before Jeremiah could bring himself to ask, he realized his treasure sock seemed lighter. Heart knocking, he poured his mother's bits of jewelry into his lap. The boy wasn't all that was missing. His six dollars were gone too.

Four

Suker raced down the dusty streets, torn between duty and pleasure. Miss Greer Tims was expecting her right after school. But today she'd found scraps of colored construction paper in the trash bin behind the school. She wanted to rush right home and make ornaments for the tree.

Not that she *had* a tree. No, Sophie wasn't giving an inch. There simply was no money, she said. So Suker'd hung her hopes on a bit of Scripture: "Ask, and ye shall receive." She was asking something powerful, for it had been two weeks since Razz's letter'd arrived, and he still hadn't come. She was asking for a tree, too. And a Christmas with some fuss.

Not wanting to jinx herself by disobeying, Suker turned in at Miss Tims's gate. There'd been a dust storm yesterday. Miss Tims had swept every room and was tuckered out. Suker beat her rugs, carried out the ashes, and fetched coal from the coal shed. Breathless from hurrying, she asked, "That all, Miss Tims?"

Thoughtfully, the old spinster pinched the loose wattle

beneath her chin. "I'd like a few potatoes. They're in the room off to the left." She waved a blue-veined hand toward the door leading down to the basement.

Suker took the enamel basin. She propped the door open as there was no light in the basement room Miss Tims had indicated. Even then, it was hard to see into the potato box. The potatoes were starting to sprout. Their stubby eyes jutted out like stiff, prickly worms.

"Bring the larger ones, Susan," Miss Greer Tims called from the top of the stairs.

Dutifully, Suker felt about for some large ones. Her fingers went right through something soft and squishy. "Phew!" she complained, for it stank something awful.

A shiver chased down her spine as she thought of the old gossips' talk. It was the ripest of smells. It *could* be a moldering body. A scurrying sound sent her heart racing. She dashed headlong up the stairs and plowed right into Miss Tims.

Miss Tims tottered this way, then that. The basin of potatoes flew out of Suker's hands as she reached out to steady the old spinster.

"I declare, Susan!" Miss Tims cried, once she had a chair beneath her. "Whatever possessed you to tear up the stairs that way?"

"I heard something scurry. Something like a . . . like a . . . like a rat . . ." Suker's voice trailed off. Feeling foolish for letting her imagination run amuck, she crawled around on the floor, collecting the scattered potatoes.

"It was only a mouse, I'm sure," said Miss Tims, who would never own up to having rats. She pointed to the bright-colored scraps littering the floor behind

Suker, adding, "You've spilled something out of your pockets."

Hesitant to soil her papers, Suker asked, "Can I wash my hands first?"

"Yes, you *may.*" Miss Tims emphasized the correct word.

It was a trap, of course. Once Suker'd washed her hands, Miss Tims wanted her to help peel the potatoes. So she sat at the table and peeled while Miss Tims quizzed her about the paper scraps.

"You dug in the trash?" she echoed, when Suker told her how she'd come across her little treasure.

"Yes, ma'am. They were at the very bottom. Billy Brisco and Martin Webb held me by the ankles so I could reach in."

Miss Tims's mouth wrinkled up like a prune. "What were you doing in the company of older boys?"

"Nothing," said Suker. "They was helping me, that's all."

"They *were,*" Miss Tims corrected. "I saw you picking up coal with them the other day, too."

"So?" said Suker. "It's just lying there, free."

"I was speaking of the inappropriateness of a young girl tagging along after older boys."

Suker could have put her mind at ease. Billy had an old car he and Martin were trying to get running. They were at the station a lot, dickering part prices with Dave. They hadn't complained more'n a little when she'd followed them down the tracks.

"It's no fun, picking up coal alone," she said by way of explanation.

"Why is it, Susan, that you haven't cultivated friend-

31

ships with any of the young ladies in your class at school?"

"I dunno," said Suker.

"You don't know," corrected Miss Tims.

Suker slid her a sidelong glance. "Maybe because they're so durn fussy," she said, though the girls in her class weren't all that fussy. They just didn't interest her much.

Miss Tims flicked a bit of potato skin off her knobby knuckles. "I'm afraid, Susan, that you put yourself in a compromising position, following after those boys."

Indignant, Suker jutted out her chin and said boldly, "You really *don't* like boys, do you?"

Miss Tims's dark eyes flashed. "If you're going to be insolent, just pick yourself up and go home."

Suker gathered up her coat and her paper scraps and did just that. Old stick, she fumed as she stormed across the yard. Trying to make it sound off-color, her picking up coal with the boys. She tramped through the house to the kitchen where Sophie was rattling a pan on the stove.

"Thanks for the ash dumping. Thanks for the coal. Thanks for sticking your hand in old rotten potatoes." Suker vented her feelings.

Sophie put a lid on the frying apples. "Miss Tims feeling her oats today, was she?"

"She's a nosey old stick and I'm not going back!" Suker declared.

"We'll see," Sophie murmured.

"All the work I've done, I've paid over and over for that dinky little handful of cherries!" Suker cried.

"Course you have," said Sophie. "But you got to see

past her crust. She's old, Suker. She needs the help and she's too proud to ask. It wouldn't be neighborly to let her fend for herself, now would it? Besides, you're medicine to her soul. You give her something to think about."

Much as they tangled, it was a wonder the old stick had any thinker left! Flash-in-the-pan temper cooling, Suker set the table. Looking around, she saw that Sophie'd blacked the stove and rubbed the nickel trim to a bright shine. She'd swept and mopped and washed away every trace of yesterday's dust storm. The whole downstairs gleamed, company bright. All at once, a new thought struck. Could it be she'd convinced Sophie? That Sophie'd done all this hard work in anticipation of Razz's visit?

The more Suker looked around, the more reasonable it seemed. There were freshly starched doilies on the arms and chair backs in the front room. The potbellied stove was shining too. And there was a scenic picture cut from a magazine, covering an ugly stain on the wall.

It cheered Suker so that she grabbed the broom and swept the front porch as clean as one could sweep in the twilight. A pair of headlights shone down the street. The car kept coming, not stopping until it'd reached their house.

A man climbed out and came toward the porch. As he drew nearer, Suker saw that he was tall and sturdily built with a confident way of carrying himself. Puzzled by a vague familiarity, she stood motionless as he paused at the bottom of the steps, waiting for him to speak. His smile flashed in the fading light. "Hello there! I'm looking for Sophie Campbell. Sophie Tilton, that is."

The door opened behind Suker before she got out a word.

"Bryce? Well, I declare, it *is* you!" Sophie stepped out on the porch, drying her hands on her apron as she came.

"Sophie!" The man took the steps in a bound. Ignoring Sophie's outstretched hand, he flung his arms around her, crying, "Aren't you a sight for sore eyes!"

There was a light in the window next door. Suker saw the curtain stir and wondered what Miss Greer Tims was making of this hugging business.

"Where is he? You *did* bring him, didn't you?" asked Sophie.

"Sure, I brought him. He's in the car," said Bryce. "But I'm afraid he's not going to remember you."

"Knew when I wrote he wouldn't. But it doesn't change my feelings none," Sophie said stoutly. Stepping out of the fellow's arms, she indicated Suker. "This is our girl, Suker. Suker, you remember Mr. Bishop, don't you? I worked for his daddy back in Shirley."

Suker gave a nod as it all fell together. Bryce Bishop! He'd come all the way from Shirley! All at once, she caught her breath. Could it be ... was there a chance ... a letter—Sophie'd written a letter. Her heart started pounding so hard, she could barely breathe.

She jumped down the steps and tore toward the car, gaining confidence with each stride. Bryce Bishop'd brought Razz along too! He was hiding! That was it! Teasing, thinking it was a fine joke. Starting to laugh herself, she jerked the door open.

"Razz? I know you're in here! You come out now!"

34

The little boy sitting there had eyes like a frightened fawn. As she leaned in to look over the seat, he shrank away from her, retreating to the far door.

Sophie came down the path after her, scolding, "Suker! What's got into you? Back away from there, you're scaring him!"

Five

They were eating in the dining room, off Sophie's best dishes. Suker sat quietly as Bryce Bishop talked and heaped his bowl with pea soup made from milk and onion and Sophie's last can of peas.

"Of course, I'd read how hard hit people were out this way what with worn-out soil, no rain, and a depression underway." He went right on telling the folks about his trip. "But nothing I'd heard could have prepared me for such godforsaken country!"

Had God cleared out of Oklahoma? Was that the trouble? He wasn't around to hear her asking? Suker'd taken a good prowl through the touring car, once Sophie showed her company inside. Razz was not in it. Even now, a good while later, the disappointment sat in her stomach like a piece of half-chewed meat.

Eating sparingly to leave plenty for her company, Sophie took only a slice of bread and half a portion of soup. "Folks have been having a hard time, sure enough."

"Some are cutting their losses and clearing out," Dave added. "Headin' west to greener pastures."

"We saw some cars packed up with everything but the garden gate." Bryce gave his head a shake as if to shed the memory. He nudged his little brother. "You'd better eat up, chum. There never was a better cook than Sophie."

The little boy just kept working the loose tooth with his tongue. He'd come in wrinkled and soiled from four days on the road. But despite the wear, his tweed knickers and matching jacket were about as fine as Suker'd ever seen on a boy in these parts. Except for John Paul Ritchie's, and his daddy was an oil man. This little lad had a grand name, too—Jeremiah Bishop the Second.

"At least drink your milk." The boy's big brother tried again.

Sophie, who'd never before been one for coddling, asked, "Would you like a little cream in it?"

Jeremiah tucked his chin, brown eyes downcast. When Maggie set to coaxing him to try the bread, he buried his face against his brother's coat sleeve. And there it stayed until Dave started telling about last week's bank robbery over in Sleepy River.

"Was anyone hurt?" asked Bryce, spoon halfway to his mouth.

"Nope. But the fella got clean away with over three hundred dollars." Dave poured a little cream into his coffee and gave it a stir. "Description fit that of Charles Arthur Floyd."

"Pretty Boy," Suker piped up, for "Pretty Boy" Floyd had robbed enough banks in Oklahoma to become a household name.

Sophie sniffed. "Nothing purty about taking what others have earned by the sweat of their brow."

"It isn't just banks and post offices he robs. He's stopped cars on the highway and robbed folks in broad daylight. At gunpoint!" said Maggie.

"I'm mighty careful at the garage. Try not to keep more'n a few dollars on hand for making change." Dave slurped his hot coffee.

This was all old news to Suker. Master Jeremiah the Second was of more immediate interest. Now that the attention was off him, he was slurping his soup, being careful of the tooth. It set her to thinking of a time her daddy'd coaxed a loose tooth out of Razz's mouth. She sopped up the soup in her bowl with the last bit of bread, then slid out of her chair.

Off in the kitchen Suker found a ball of string in Sophie's catchall drawer. The door leading out to the wash porch'd do just fine. She tied one end of the string to the knob, then went back into the dining room where the grown-ups were finishing their coffee. She sidled around behind the boy's chair.

"I got something to show you," she whispered. After a moment or two, Jeremiah the Second followed her out to the kitchen.

"You want that tooth pulled?" Suker asked.

He chewed on the cuff of one shirt sleeve, eyes downcast.

She linked her arms across her flat chest. "Well, do you?"

"Will it hurt?" He spoke his first words since entering the house.

"That depends. You a baby?"

He wagged his head.

38

"Then it ain't more'n you can tolerate. Open your mouth," said Suker. Watching him struggle with himself, she hummed a baby lullabye like Razz used to do when she was slow to see things his way. Jeremiah the Second scrunched his eyes shut and dropped his jaw.

"You'll be glad to get rid of this nuisance," Suker assured him as she tied the string snug to the tooth. She motioned for him to back up until the string was stretched full-length. Then she crossed to the door and opened it inward. This made for a bit of slack in the string.

"Now what you've got to do is take a small step back and hang onto the table, there. That's it," she said as he grabbed hold of the table. "Ready now? Here goes."

Ca-whop! she slammed the door. Jeremiah Bishop the Second smothered a yelp. The tooth was still hanging, but now it jutted out at an unnatural angle.

"Whoops." Chagrined, Suker scratched her head. "Back up and we'll try it again."

But it was not to be. Sophie came in from the dining room with an armload of dishes. She stopped short, sized up the situation in a glance, and turned a stern eye on Suker. "I declare, child, what're you thinkin'?"

Stung by her accusing tone, Suker protested, "I was only tryin' to help."

"Oh, well, yes! This is a heap of help." Sophie cut the string with a knife, pulled out a chair, and lifted the boy onto her lap. "That's a brave boy. We'll fix you right up."

Suker could see blood outlining his little white teeth. Edging closer, she asked, "You gonna pull it?"

"Get a clean rag, then go back to the dining room and

39

clear the dishes. Rob'll be here soon, and Maggie'll fuss if you keep them waiting."

Even though Sophie's tone had softened some, Suker went about her chore, feeling injured. Wasn't like she'd *meant* to hurt the little prince! Oh well. At least she had pageant practice to look forward to. Rob and Maggie were helping the choir director work with the children. And tonight, after practice, they were to decorate the church Christmas tree.

The men had just adjourned to the front room when Rob Kelsey came, scrubbed clean and wearing his only suit. He was a few years older than Maggie, though not as old as Bryce Bishop nor as stout and handsome either. But he stretched a couple inches taller when Maggie slipped her arm through his and introduced him as her special fella.

"Got your lines down pat?" Dave asked Suker with a smile.

Suker put on a hard face and said with a shooing motion, " 'No room'."

"She's the innkeeper," explained Maggie for Bryce Bishop's benefit. "Run get your coat and tell Mama we're going."

Suker swept the last coffee cup off the table on her way through the dining room. Sophie was standing on a chair, reaching for a round tin on a high shelf.

"Rob's here, and we're going."

"All right. You remember to thank Mrs. Nethers," Sophie added. "She's working awful hard to help you children with that pageant."

The boy was sitting at the table, admiring the pearly white tooth in his hand. Suker paused, thinking of telling him she hadn't meant to hurt him. But it was hard to find the words. "Keep your tongue out of the hole, and you'll grow a gold tooth," she whispered in his ear.

Overhearing, Sophie said, "Hush, Suker, that ain't true." Then she popped the lid off the tin and offered the boy a cookie.

Suker couldn't name when they'd last had cookies. Mouth watering, she waited real patient-like, till Sophie passed the tin her way. "Help yourself, before the men get at 'em," she said.

Feeling a mite happier, Suker politely took just one.

"You can have one more," said Sophie.

So she ate one quick and took the second up to her room. She'd eat it later—real slow, relishing every single bite.

The angels, from the tiniest tot up to girls as old as Suker, were up front practicing when Suker, Rob, and Maggie arrived at the church. The choir director, Mrs. Nethers, motioned for Maggie to take over. A little bitty woman with the energy of a threshing machine, she got Rob to one side and rattled off something in his ear.

"What'd she want?" asked Suker, as Mrs. Nethers went to the head of the basement stairs and shouted for the shepherds and wise men to come up.

"The church board turned down her request for a pine tree," Rob murmured. "No money."

"What? No tree?" yelped Suker. "I thought we were going to decorate."

"We are," said Rob, slipping back into his coat. "Just won't be a traditional Christmas tree. Tell Maggie I'll be back in a bit."

Mystified, Suker watched him leave.

"Suker? Come on up here," called Mrs. Nethers. She

41

clapped her hands for order and shouted over the children's voices, "Quiet now, children. Line up. We're going to run through the whole pageant, start to finish."

They ran through it twice, and even then it was pretty rough in places. But Mrs. Nethers wasn't easily discouraged. She settled the children in the front pews and impressed upon them what an important thing they were doing.

"As you know," she said, "lots of folks have had it pretty rough this year. You see a lot of long, worried faces. But we're bringing them hope. We're bringing them Christmas!"

Rob, Billy, and Martin came in while she was talking. Each of them had a tumbleweed.

One little boy raised his hand. "Are we going to decorate now?"

"Yes, we are," said Mrs. Nethers. She smiled real bright. "Now, we couldn't get a cedar tree this year. But that's not going to stop us! No, sir! We're going to have a very special tree. One that shows imagination!"

Her enthusiasm worked like magic on the younger children. They were delighted with the idea of sticking tumbleweeds together for a tree. And even Suker had to admit the weed tree sparkled kind of pretty when they'd wet it down and sprinkled it with salt.

Colored bows and buttons and angel chains cut from butcher paper served as decorations. It was a brave effort at least. But Suker couldn't help missing the scent of cedar and the prickle of fresh needles. She wasn't the only one, either.

"Don't seem right, somehow," muttered Billy. He and Martin had hitched a ride home with them.

"If the church had a real tree, folks'd feel a touch of Christmas," said Martin, as they chugged past John Paul Ritchie's lighted house.

Suker could hear the hum of the Delco generator above the cough and sputter of Rob's cold truck. Admiring the fine two-story house, she said, "Must be nice to have lots of money."

Billy arched his neck, looking back at the house. "Come to think of it, Mr. Ritchie could donate a tree. It wouldn't break the bank."

"Yes, and then folks would say he was showing off," said Maggie, who'd inherited a good dose of Sophie's fairness. "They didn't have cedar trees in Bethlehem, either."

"For a fact? You sure?" asked Martin.

"Course I'm sure! Now cheer up, before you drag Suker down with all your gloomy talk," scolded Maggie as they bumped on down the street.

Wedged in so tight, there was hardly room to shiver, Suker appreciated the thought. It was the most notice anyone'd given her since the little prince had arrived.

Suker trotted along behind as Rob saw Maggie to the door. Dave and Sophie were entertaining Bryce Bishop in the front room. The potbellied stove, so often left cold these days, was putting out a nice warm glow. Suker plunked down on the hassock at Dave's feet.

But Sophie shooed her off, saying, "It's past yer bedtime, Suker. Your gown's in the kitchen. Go on and wash up."

Suker sighed and said good night. She made short work of her washup. With the light of the kitchen behind her, Suker plodded surefooted up the shadowy staircase, across the landing, and into her dark room.

The cookie was right where she'd left it. But just as she reached for it, a small rustling noise quickened her pulse. She strained her ears. Was that the light whisper of breathing? Yes, feather light! A tingle crept up her spine. Someone was hiding in her room!

Heart pounding, Suker was out the door and across the landing in the stroke of an eyelash. All at once, she stopped short. *Could it be Razz?* Laughing at her most likely! Getting a big kick out of scaring her.

Hope casting out fear, Suker crept back across the threshold, whispering, "Razz? That you?"

Six

───◆───

Suker teetered between joy and fear, waiting for an answer. When none came, she ran her hand along the lamp stand. Her fingers closed over the matches. Hastily, she struck one. The small yellow flame extinguished both hope and fear. It wasn't Razz teasing. It was Jeremiah Bishop the Second curled up in her bed!

Atop the covers, a dimpled hand cradled her doll, Clarisse. Suker wanted nothing to do with him, least of all to pity him. Yet, there he lay, tear stains on his face, mouth gaping open as he slept, showing the hole where his tooth had been.

Suker blew out the match just before it singed her fingers. Leaving Clarisse behind, she took her cookie to Maggie's room. It was warmer than usual, thanks to the fire in the potbellied stove below. Suker hunkered down on the black iron grate. She munched her cookie and listened to the grown-ups talk.

"Friends have invited me to stay with them," Bryce

Bishop was saying. "But their house is small and they have no children of their own."

Dave's voice rumbled low.

"I wish I could say when it'll be," Bryce Bishop replied. "But I just don't know how long it'll take me to find a job and make a new start."

"Take all the time you need. He'll be fine—don't you worry." Sophie's words carried clear as a bell.

"Thanks, Sophie. You too Dave. When a fellow loses his money, he sure learns in a hurry his true-blue friends."

An uneasy suspicion stirred in Suker's head. He wasn't *leaving* the little prince, surely! Dave spoke again, so softly Suker couldn't make out his words. There was a slight pause, then the conversation shifted to other things. She finished her cookie and licked the crumbs from her fingers, savoring the sweetness.

Footsteps on the stairs gave all too brief a warning. Suker plowed beneath Maggie's covers. She pulled her head in like a turtle as candlelight preceded Sophie into Maggie's room.

"Thought that must be you, dropping cookie crumbs down the grate." Sophie folded the quilts back to reveal Suker's guilt-stricken face. She wagged her head. "Eavesdroppin' on grown-ups. What've you got to say for yourself?"

"I was just warming myself on the grate," Suker fibbed.

Sophie's mouth tightened. "Don't go digging yerself a deeper ditch, telling tales."

Flushing, Suker admitted, "All right. I was listening." When Sophie didn't jump right in with another rebuke,

46

she asked, "How long is that boy figuring on sleepin' in my bed?"

"It isn't Jere's choice, Suker," said Sophie in a level voice. "Fact is, he doesn't know himself, yet."

"Then his brother *is* leaving him here?" Suker asked.

Sophie nodded. "For the time being. Until he finds a job. And a decent place to live. You don't mind giving up your bed for a while, do you?"

Suker worried a piece of quilt between thumb and forefinger. Thoughts with jagged edges tumbled around in her head. It wasn't so much the bed, for she liked snuggling up next to Maggie. But she didn't want him taking her place in Sophie's heart, or Dave's or Maggie's either.

"You can make room for him, can't you?" Sophie pressed.

Suker wasn't real sure that she could. But that wasn't what Sophie wanted to hear. Finally, she said in a small voice, "I thought maybe Razz had come with them."

Sophie's hand was warm on Suker's brow as she smoothed back her hair. "I'm real sorry you got your hopes dashed, Suker. Seems being away from our loved ones hurts most at Christmas."

Suker refused to give in to the rise of tears. Setting her chin, she said, "He'll come. It ain't Christmas yet. I been praying about it."

Sophie hesitated, a struggle on her face. Picking her words with care, she said, "That's right, Suker. You just keep it up. I hope you'll mention the little one, too, before you say your amen."

The boy again. Suker flounced over on her side as Sophie retreated with the candle. He was snug asleep in her bed. With her doll. And her folks pitying him so. Would he go to the garage next and stand on her pop crate behind the counter? What about her place at the table? How was she to hold on to what was her own?

Suker closed her eyes, thinking of her cat, Sassy, back in Illinois and a little hound dog pup her daddy'd brought home. Sassy'd spit and hissed and scratched that pup's nose, letting him know right off who was boss. Within weeks, the pup was bigger than the cat. But he'd learned his place. Though he loved nothing better than treeing the barn cats, that pup never once offered to chase Sassy. She'd secured her position.

Maybe there *was* room for Jeremiah Bishop the Second. Just so long as he understood that Suker Tucker the one-and-only was here first, last, and forever. First off, he'd best be taught about leaving his hands off what belonged to her. Suker slipped out of bed. Resolutely, she padded along the icy floor to collect her doll, Clarisse, from the little hound-pup prince.

Jeremiah dreamed of afternoon tea with his mother. The bread was warm from the oven. It dripped with butter and black raspberry jam. The delicious yeasty smell seemed so real, he sniffed and stretched and opened his eyes. Sunlight burned away the misty dream. He was in a strange bed in a strange room in a strange house. The air was so cold, he could see his breath. Where was Bryce? He bolted upright. But the sound of Bryce's voice drifted from the kitchen below, stilling his racing heart.

The cold floor stung Jeremiah's bare feet. He pulled on his wool knickers. Where were his stockings and shirt? He got down on his knees and peeked beneath the bed.

"What're you looking for?"

The freckle-faced girl with the whispy yellow hair was watching him from the doorway. Jeremiah's tongue found the hole where his tooth had come out.

"Now you've done it. No gold tooth." The girl thrust her hands into the pockets of her bib overalls. She rocked back on the run-down heels of her shoes.

"My socks are gone," he said.

"Saturday's Sophie's wash day," said the girl in her scratchy-flat voice. "Suker," that's what they called her.

"Is she washing my shirt too?"

"Probably. She washes everything that isn't buttoned up tight." Toes pointing inward, Suker came across the room and nudged his suitcase with her foot. "Haven't you got another shirt?"

He hadn't thought of that.

"I'll get it for you," she offered.

Jeremiah stood by watching as she pawed through his suitcase with curious fingers. She handed him stockings and a clean shirt.

"Too good to play in. But then, so are the rest of them. Your folks got money, I'll wager."

"They're dead." He tried saying it out loud. It hurt his heart, as if he'd called them a bad word.

"Mine, too. But I got a brother," she said. "He's coming to see me."

Razz, the boy who'd taken his money. She was wrong. He wasn't coming. He wouldn't tell her, though. It might make her mad, and he didn't want that.

"After we eat, you can dump the ashes and feed the

chickens while I check-see on Miss Greer Tims next door. Then, if you want, you can help me glue up some paper scraps for Christmas ornaments," she said as he finished dressing.

Jeremiah doubted they'd be staying that long. Bryce was anxious to get to that place called California. He stuffed his feet into his shoes and stole quietly down the stairs after her.

Sophie and Maggie were scurrying around the kitchen. Bryce was alone at the table, smoking a cigarette. His plate was empty, and so was his coffee cup. Jeremiah got a queer, jittery feeling in his stomach. He scarcely heard Sophie greet him, or Maggie either.

"Are we going now?" he asked Bryce, who was dressed to travel.

"Here in a bit," said Bryce. "Sit down and eat a bite, Jere."

There was an uneasy wrinkle in his brother's smile. Pressure built in Jeremiah's chest. Upstairs, dreaming of bread, his belly was gurgling. Now it was sour. "I'm not hungry," he said in a whisper.

"Now, now. You'll hurt Maggie's feelings. She baked this bread especially for you," said Bryce.

The dark-haired girl with the pretty hazel eyes slid a warm slice onto a plate and set it in front of him. She patted his shoulder, then turned away saying, "I'm going now, Mama. Why don't you help me, Suker, so I don't have to make two trips?"

Suker grumbled she hadn't had any breakfast. But she grabbed a slice of bread. Then she picked up one of the baskets of fresh-baked loaves and left with Maggie. There was a closed-in porch just off the kitchen. Sophie

50

headed that way with a bucket of water hot off the stove.

"I'll be out here washing if you need me," she said. Then she closed the door quietly.

Jeremiah's throat felt dry. He tried to eat, but the bread made a hard knot at the back of his throat.

Bryce knocked the ash off his cigarette. "Listen, chum. California's a long way yet and I know you're tired of traveling."

Jeremiah stopped chewing. He blinked, waiting for him to go on.

"There's a good chance you won't like it once we get there. So I've been thinking . . . that is, Sophie and Dave have offered . . ." Bryce stopped. He crushed out the cigarette and ran a hand through his jet-black hair.

Jeremiah felt like crying without knowing why. He scraped his chair back. "I'll get my coat."

"No, wait." Bryce caught his arm. He lifted him onto his lap. "Maybe the best way to say this is straight out. Dave and Sophie have invited you to stay here a while. So I'm going on to California alone, Jere."

His coat. He had to get his coat. Jeremiah struggled to get free. But Bryce hung on, talking faster. "Once I get there, I'll find a job and a house, then I'll send for you. Now, I don't want you to worry, chum. It's not going to be that long, before we're together again."

Panic burned Jeremiah's chest. Tears pressed for release. "I want to come too."

"No. Not just yet, Jere. This is hard, I know. But it's for the best," said Bryce.

Bryce's big arms closed around him. He smelled of

soap and tobacco and medicine. It was all happening too fast. There were no words to fight him. Hot tears spilled down Jeremiah's cheeks. He sat like a stone, hugging nothing but hurt and crying for his mother.

Seven

Highway 66 went straight through the middle of Clement. But the railroad tracks skirted along the northern edge of town, passing within a stone's throw of Suker's house. After carrying the basket to the station for Maggie, Suker took the tracks home. The air was brisk, but the sun was bright. A coal train had gone through in the night, losing a bit of its cargo. She filled her pockets, then skidded down the steep embankment into her own backyard.

The chickens cocked their heads and criticized her tardiness. Suker scattered feed and filled their water jars. Glorying in its being Saturday, she forgot Razz for a moment and Jeremiah Bishop the Second. She was gathering eggs and whistling off-key when a shriek ripped the still morning air. Jeremiah!

Suker tore around the side of the house. He was trying to get into his coat as he ran screaming after his brother's departing car. But he had the coat upside down. It threw him off balance. He tripped and skidded facedown along frosty ruts. Sophie came running out to where he lay sobbing.

Suker turned her eyes away. A heavy pressure on her chest, she went back to the chickens and finished her chores. The closed-in back porch was steamy with Sophie's washing. She left the eggs there and her lumps of coal. Then she scuffed across the backyard to check-see on Miss Greer Tims.

"You've got company," said Miss Tims.

Suker said flat out, "His name's Jeremiah Bishop. Sophie used to work for his folks back in Illinois. But they're dead now. So he's staying with us a spell."

"I see." Miss Tims stroked her thin wattle. "Who was the man with him?"

"That's Bryce, his older brother."

Miss Tims's mouth pursed up like a prune. "A brother? Why isn't he caring for the boy?"

Suker shrugged. "Shiftless, I guess."

Miss Tims accepted that with a nod. "It's the nature of men. I had five brothers myself. But do you think any of them helped me when our ailing father needed care?"

Suker knew for a fact they hadn't. Miss Tims had told her so often enough. But she looked as if she expected an answer, so she said, "Ain't likely."

"Isn't, Susan. *Isn't.* Why do you persist in saying 'ain't'?"

"I forget." Sometimes, she remembered but said it anyway. "Did you want the ashes emptied?"

Miss Tims wanted them dumped. She also wanted the particulars on Jeremiah and his dead parents and his run-off-to-California brother. The only reason Suker stayed was she didn't want to go home. Not with Jeremiah Bishop the Second so broken-down beside himself.

Miss Tims ran out of chores about the same time Suker ran out of answers. There was nothing to do but go home. She let herself in the back porch. Sophie had her hair tied up in a rag. Her face glistened with sweat as she cranked the wringer handle, running Dave's overalls through the rinse tub.

"Miss Tims feeling poorly?" she asked.

"Nope. Just contrary and nosey as all get out," said Suker.

Sophie was one for minding her own business. She grimaced but let it go, saying, "Ask Jere if he'd like to help string up this wash."

The boy was at the table, sitting so still, pigeons could have roosted on him. He had a red scratch and a bruised cheek from his fall.

"We're going to hang up the wash. Want to come out with us?" Suker asked.

He didn't say a word.

"You could hand us the pegs," she added.

He still didn't stir.

"That's all right, Suker. We'll manage," Sophie said from the doorway.

It went like that all morning. The boy ate a bite at lunch, then was too long in the privy. Sophie got concerned and went to see about him. They came back together, the front of him all soiled where he'd lost his lunch. He was so pale and pitiful, Suker forgot all about Sassy and the hound pup. Once Sophie'd cleaned him up, she invited him to sit down with her and paste up some colored-paper scraps.

"You stir the paste," she said, having put a little flour

and warm water in a dish. He wouldn't, so she did it herself.

"See what I'm doing here? Just piece them together on this brown paper. Then, when it dries, we'll cut out some ornaments. Bells, angels, candles—stuff like that. We're going to have to see about a Christmas tree, too."

Suker slid him a glance. He sat with his dimpled hands between the table and his chin, not saying a word. "We can't buy a real one," she went on. "So we're going to have to substitute. We used tumbleweeds at church. Wasn't half bad."

He kept right on wearing the same bleak brown gaze. It riled her a bit, and she started humming a lullabye. He didn't even blink. The paste dried on Suker's fingers. She gave them a rinse and came back to the table, done with being polite.

"Your brother ought not to have left you." She went straight to the point. "If it was me, I'd be mad as a hornet. But then, Miss Tims says it's the nature of men to be shiftless and selfish. So you'd just as well get over feeling sorry."

Sophie frowned a clear message.

Suker sighed and gave up trying to get Jeremiah Bishop the Second to talk. Leaving her paper-scrap quilt to dry, she grabbed her coat. "I'm going to gather coal off the tracks."

The sun was still shining, but clouds were moving in and the air was growing colder. Halfway across the yard, Suker looked back to see the boy following. The embankment was thick with winter-white weeds. Seeing him hesitate, Suker held out her hand and pulled him up after her.

Jeremiah didn't say a word. But he kept hold of her

hand until she broke free to pick up a piece of coal. "I came along here this morning and filled my pockets in no time," she said, turning west toward the station.

Jeremiah picked up three rocks for every piece of coal. Suker showed him the difference, and after that he did better. But he wasn't a bit more wordy than he'd been all day.

Dave was gassing up a car at the station. She waved and kept going, proud to be of help, finding free coal. The soles of her shoes were thin. The colder her feet became, the more the rocks seemed to jab. She relieved the tenderness by walking on the rail.

"These boys I know have contests," she said, thinking of Billy Brisco and Martin Webb. "Each one of 'em gets on a rail. Then they duel with sticks, seeing who can stay railed the longest. Here, take the bucket," she said, for it was hard staying balanced, what with being pigeon-toed.

About every ten steps, Suker slipped off. But she kept trying until she felt a faint vibration through her shoes. Way down the tracks, just a dot on the horizon, a train was coming.

"We gotta clear off." Suker took the bucket from Jeremiah and led him down the weedy embankment to safety. Cold as it was, they needed to keep moving to stay warm. But she loved trains and couldn't resist watching the dot grow into a slow-moving freight. The big stacks belched smoke. She thought of Sophie's wash, and hoped she'd get it down before the train blew cinders all over it. The ground rumbled beneath her feet.

Jeremiah slipped his hand into hers and tugged. His cheeks were bright red and he was starting to shiver. But she still dallied. "Let's count the cars."

A couple of wanderers were riding along in an empty boxcar. They sat smoking, legs dangling out the yawning door. They were gray whiskered and wrinkled about the eyes. A third fella, no older than Billy and Martin, was riding on top of a coal car. Seeing them standing there with a bucket, he started kicking off coal.

Jeremiah jerked on her hand. He looked so startled, she asked, "What's the matter?"

He said something, but the train was too loud. "What?" she yelled and bent her ear low.

He pointed down the tracks. The fella on the coal car was climbing down a side ladder. He flung down his sack, jumped clear of the train and hit the ground rolling. Suker caught her breath as he scrambled to his feet, retrieved his flour sack pack, and came loping back toward them.

She stirred uneasily. "Best go." But something about the way he carried himself sent her heart slamming into her chest. No, couldn't be, for in her mind was a smooth-cheeked boy with hair like a bird's nest and a cunning grin. Why, this fella was tall as a man.

It was just her wanting it so. Twice now, she'd set herself up, only to be let down again. Anyway, if Razz was riding the rails, he'd come from the east, not the west.

And yet Suker's heart insisted. She stumbled back toward the tracks and stood staring. The man kept coming, grinning now like a clever young fox.

Eight

————◆————

Suker stood rooted in wonderment, knowing, yet fearful to the very last moment, of being mistaken. The fella reached her just as the last train car rumbled past.

"Don't you know me?"

"Razz! It *is* you!" Suker forgot in her joy that Razz and her daddy'd never been much for open affection. She flung her arms around him.

" 'Course it's me! Didn't you get my letter?" Grinning, Razz disentangled himself.

"Sure I got it. But I'd just about given up hope!"

"See here, Suker. Seven hundred-odd miles on empty pockets is no easy trick." Razz turned out his pocket linings, waving Hoover flags.

Suker laughed, all the while noting the changes in her brother. His face was longer than she remembered, and thinner too. The whiskers peppering his cheeks and his chin sure made him look grown-up. But his eyes, which could flash from laughter to sly mischief to lock-jawed

59

resentment, were just as arresting as ever. She hugged herself to keep from hugging him again.

"Nothing can keep Christmas from coming now! Did you come all the way by train? Bet you overshot Clement, didn't you?"

He confessed it with a sheepish grin. "Found myself in Texas, come daylight."

"That's what threw me! Your being on an eastbound train."

"It's a little hard to recognize a place you've never been, smarty. Partic'larly when you're sleeping." Razz grinned and rubbed her head.

"Was it an awful trial, that long ride?" she asked anxiously.

"Wasn't so bad, really. I came most of the way with Bryce Bishop."

"You *did?*" She ducked out of reach before he Dutch-rubbed her bald headed.

"Sure did. Until yesterday afternoon when he dumped me out."

"Well, I'll be. What'd he dump you for?"

Razz shrugged it off lightly, saying, "I gave Bryce a bottle of 'shine in trade for a ride. Once it was empty, he got quarrelsome."

Sensing an evasion, Suker frowned. "How do you mean?"

"He was afraid my visit coinciding with his might put a hitch in his plan, that's all."

"What plan?"

"To dump Jere on Sophie and Dave, of course."

Suker's jaw dropped. It went over her again worse than fingernails on a chalkboard, Jeremiah's stricken

60

wails. "You mean he planned all along to leave Jeremiah with us?"

Razz nodded. He picked up the flour sack containing his belongings. A piece of twine served as a drawstring. He pulled it snug and glanced toward the roadside where Jeremiah waited.

"Two extra mouths to feed in times hard as these *is* burdensome. Sophie and Dave don't have to worry about me, though. I won't overstay my welcome," he added quickly.

"I still can't believe Bryce Bishop booted you out." Suker tooted out her mouth like a horn. "I declare, what a shiftless, selfish lout! Miss Tims says it's the nature of men."

Razz snorted, half amused, half defensive. "Who's Miss Tims?"

"An old maid, lives next door. She caught me swiping cherries off her tree, and now I have to do chores for her." Suker jammed her hands into her pockets. "The highway's easier walking. Let's go to the garage and warm up."

Razz followed her through the weeds toward Highway 66. He aimed a big grin at Jeremiah. "Hello there, Jere. I see you've met my sister."

Jeremiah cold-shouldered Razz, looking right at him but not saying a word.

"He's not much of a talker," Suker said quickly.

"Oh, I don't know about that. We had a good talk the other night. We're traveling pals, aren't we, Jere?" Razz tried again.

Jeremiah passed Suker the coal bucket, still bent on ignoring Razz. Resisting the urge to mediate, Suker

61

closed numb fingers around the handle. But Razz snatched it from her.

"I'll carry that. Tomorrow, you might want to come out a bit further. I've been kicking coal off for the past mile."

"You steal," said Jeremiah.

Suker stopped, surprised. Not only that he'd spoken, but at the heat in his voice.

Razz gave a short laugh. "There's tons of it. They aren't going to miss a bucket or two."

Jeremiah's mittened hand slipped into Suker's. He entreated her with trusting brown eyes. "He took my money."

Suker sucked in a frigid breath. "What money?"

"My dollars."

Razz hunkered down in front of Jeremiah. "You're missing some money?"

"How much?" asked Suker.

"Six dollars," said Jeremiah. He shrugged Razz's hands off his shoulders and edged away.

"Maybe you left it in your brother's car," Suker reasoned. "He drove off kind of sudden-like this morning."

"I missed it before then," said Jeremiah. He angled Razz another resentful glance. *"He* took it."

"Don't be silly. Course he didn't," Suker snapped.

Razz suggested helpfully, "Maybe it's in your suitcase with your other belongings. Shall we take a look?"

Jeremiah's eyes glittered dark in his pinched face. "It's *my* suitcase. Don't you touch it."

"No need to be so hateful. Razz is only trying to help," said Suker. For Razz's benefit, she added, "Anyway, it's not there. I would have noticed. I been all through that suitcase."

Jeremiah withdrew his hand from hers. But Suker scarcely noticed, so thrilled was she that Razz had finally come. She quickly dismissed Jeremiah's lost money, her thoughts full of Christmas. It was only eight days away. It'd be the best ever! Brittle air stinging her lungs and her hands and toes, she told Razz there'd be no Christmas tree. Least not like the ones they'd cut in the woods back home.

He shrugged. "Times are hard. Folks can't live on pine needles and tree bark."

They talked as fast as they walked, remembering past Christmases when their father was still living and they'd hung stockings and strung popcorn and looked forward to something special beneath the tree. It seemed a long time ago.

Suker glanced back to see Jeremiah had fallen behind. His head was down, his hands in his pockets. He looked so small and cold and lost, a shadow crept over her happiness. But Razz chased it away, saying, as the Flying Red Horse came into full view, "This is Dave's place? Looks pretty nice."

"It's a good spot, along Highway 66. Dave's a fine mechanic. I help out by pumping gas. I can add in my head and make change, too." Spotting Martin and Billy out front inflating a tire, Suker waved.

"Who're they?" Razz asked.

"A couple of fellas I know. Come on, I'll introduce you."

After the long walk, Jeremiah wanted to be where it was warm. But he had to talk to Suker first. Alone. So he waited for her outside the privy.

"He took it." He pointed toward the house where Razz had disappeared.

"Razz?" She hitched a coverall strap in place. "Took what?"

"My money."

"That again? It ain't so, Jere. You probably just lost it." She jerked shivering into her coat and wiped her nose with the frayed finger of one glove.

He rammed cold hands into his pockets and scowled. "If my brother was here, he'd make Razz give it back."

Fire in her eyes, she retorted, "Your brother's probably the one who took it. I wouldn't put it past him."

"He wouldn't do that. *Your* brother's the thief! He takes food, too. And coal."

"He is not a thief, and you'd better quit saying it," Suker warned. She caught the privy door as the wind snapped it back and added impatiently, "Go, if you have to. I'm freezing."

Jeremiah'd already relieved himself back at the gas station. He waited while Suker latched the door, then followed her to the house next door. She glowered at him from the top of the steps.

"You can't come in. Miss Greer Tims lives here and she don't like boys."

Jeremiah sat down on the bottom step to wait.

"She won't want you on her step either."

He was tired and cold and hungry. His chin wobbled.

"Jeremiah!" She planted a hand on a narrow hip and ordered, "Go on home."

A wave of longing swept over him. If only he could! Or to that gate, where angels sang and his parents were waiting. His eyes started leaking again.

Suker came down the steps and perched beside him.

She let out a sigh. "It won't take me long to do my chores. Saturday night's bath night. But maybe later, we can cut out some ornaments from that paper we pasted up. How's that sound?"

The sting was gone from her voice. Feeling more hopeful, he tried again. "He'd give it back if you asked him to."

She leaped right up. "Looky here, Jeremiah Bishop the Second. You jest as well get it into your head. My brother didn't take your precious money!"

Jeremiah knew that tone. His mother used it the time the hired man had accused him of throwing ripe tomatoes at the pigs. "My son wouldn't do that!" she'd said.

Mother'd believed what she wanted to believe. Suker was doing that too. He wasn't going to get any help from her.

The kitchen was warm and damp with bathwater heating and the tail end of Sophie's wash strung about. The onion soup warmed his stomach, and unlike lunch, it stayed down. Jeremiah looked on as Suker's family made Razz welcome with talk and laughter and some cream in his coffee. Suker sat beside Razz, and when his piece of bread was gone, she tore hers in half and shared it.

After dinner, Dave built a fire out in the front room. Sophie sat down at the quilt frame. Jeremiah listened as she determined the order of baths. Maggie was to go first, she said, because her boyfriend was coming. Then Suker. Then he'd have a turn. Then Razz. While Razz was behind the screen, he'd check his pockets and see if he had his six silver dollars.

It was a good plan. Jeremiah sat down in a chair to

wait. His eyes soon drooped shut. By the time they came open again, Maggie had left with her date. Razz had gone out too with the friends he'd made at the garage that afternoon. He'd have to wait now, to check his pockets.

Long faced over being left behind, Suker was sitting on the floor near the potbellied stove. She rubbed the marks the stiff scissors had made on her fingers. "Did you want to help or not?" she asked, offering Jeremiah the scissors.

Dave looked up from the book he'd just opened. "Awake now, are you? Thought you was going to miss the story."

Sophie looked up from her quilt in the corner. "Go ahead and help Suker awhile, if you'd like to, Jere. I can reheat your bathwater."

Jeremiah reached for the scissors. He traced around a cookie cutter, making the shape of a star. Suker got over being sulky as Dave read aloud from a Christmas book.

Christmas. Jeremiah remembered the party at the house last year. His mother had worn a beautiful blue gown. She'd sat on the stairs with him, listening to the music, pointing out the guests, and telling him their names. He remembered smelling the good smells drifting from the kitchen, and seeing a tree as tall and green as a forest. Bright colors had shone against the dark branches like stars gleaming from the sky. He closed his eyes and saw the dancing. He heard the laughter and recalled how he'd yearned to be a part of all that swirl and sound and color.

That was Christmas. It had nothing to do with paper decorations dusty with flour paste. Except maybe for the excitement in Suker's face. But he could not share in that either. Nor did he follow the story Dave was reading. He was numb, like a foot gone to sleep or hands so cold they'd lost all feeling.

Nine

Cinders fizzled in the potbellied stove as Dave read aloud from Dickens's *A Christmas Carol.* Suker's fingers ached from cutting. The story flowed bittersweet like sugared coffee. Sophie's taut thread plucked the quilt, punctuating pauses. Word by cut by stitch, the evening faded away. Resisting her pleas to read on, Dave marked the book, leaving Tiny Tim's family in a terrible fix.

Sophie stirred herself to see that Jeremiah had a bath. After he'd gone off to bed, Suker decided their artwork was too good to wait for a tree. She strung paper bells and trees and stars from window latches, cupboard handles, and doorknobs. She even stuck a decoration to the back of the chair where Dave now sat dozing.

On her way upstairs, Suker saw a candle burning in her bedroom. Sophie sat on the edge of the bed, brushing her hair and talking softly to Jeremiah.

Holding out the last star, Suker asked, "You want this hung on your bedpost?"

Jeremiah hastily poked something beneath the covers.

Suspicious, she asked, "What've you got?"

"He was sprucing up your doll a bit. You don't mind, do you?" asked Sophie.

Suker trotted around to the other side of the bed and threw back the covers. There lay Clarisse, a pearl pin in her hair. A hairbrush was lying there too. The memory of Sassy and the hound pup rushed over her.

"You brushed her hair!" she accused.

"He was real gentle, Suker. The pin looks nice, don't you think?"

Quick-like, Suker reached for Clarisse. "She's my doll. You should have asked me before you played with her."

Jeremiah didn't say a word. Nor did Sophie. But tiny lines drew her mouth down. She curled an arm around Jeremiah. Suker tossed her head, unclasped the pin, and carried Clarisse off to bed.

The next morning, the frosty street crunched beneath Suker's feet. She blew on her cold hands and glanced back at Dave and Sophie. They were strolling along with the little hound-pup prince between them.

"Race you!" Razz cut into her sour thoughts.

Suker tore down the street after him.

Halfway across town, they burst through the church doors. Suker choked down the noise of the race. She blinked dancing stars and hooked her coat to a peg. The folks who'd gotten there ahead of them stood up front whispering like a radio turned low. Pungent green tickled her nose. She started up the aisle, then stopped so suddenly, Razz ran over her heels. Behind the altar, stretching toward the ceiling, was a stately cedar tree!

A pouncy smile skipped across Razz's face. "Looky there! What's that dwarfing your tumbleweed tree?"

Suker could only gaze in wonder. The graceful boughs glistened fresh and green and glorious. There were no ribbons on it. No paper ornaments or buttons or baubles. Yet it towered over the gaily bedecked tumbleweed with pure, vibrant beauty. She dashed ahead for a closer look. Those standing about were all wondering the same thing—who'd bestowed on the church such a generous gift?

No one in Suker's Sunday school class knew the answer. Nor did the pastor. At the close of worship, Mrs. Nethers, the choir director, echoed the pastor's thank you to the mystery benefactor.

"What a lovely gesture! God bless you, whoever you are," she said. Then she reminded the children to come for pageant practice that evening.

As service broke up, the folks of Clement took time to meet Jeremiah and Razz. Jeremiah hung his head and wouldn't say boo. But Razz smiled and shook hands and talked so polite, Suker's chest swelled near to bursting.

"That tree sure does look pretty. Suker, why don't you take Jere up front for a closer look?" said Sophie.

Jeremiah barely glanced at the cedar tree. Instead, he stretched out a hand to touch a glittery branch of the tumbleweed tree.

"That's salt, makes it sparkle. I made that little lamb and that chain of angels, too," Suker volunteered.

Razz, Martin, and Billy soon joined them.

Razz tilted his head and teased, "Couldn't you fellas have found a tumbleweed didn't lean to the left?"

"I say we change the decorations to the big tree," said Martin.

70

Billy nodded. "Then let's haul this pitiful thing on out back and burn it."

Suker nibbled the inside of her cheek. To her relief, Maggie marched to the defense of the tumbleweed tree. "You'll do no such thing! The children decorated this tree, it belongs to them!"

Razz wrinkled his nose. "It smells like weeds."

"Leave it to a woodsman to notice!" said Maggie.

" 'Woodsman'?" A teasing glint lighted Razz's expression. "That's an improvement over 'old dumb woodsie,' I guess."

Maggie's cheeks turned pink. Razz laughed and told Martin and Billy, "Maggie and I went to grammar school together. I was the fella she loved to hate. Isn't that right, Maggie?"

"There you go, giving yourself too much credit." Maggie sniffed and turned her back on him.

Bill guffawed. Martin snickered too, and Razz's face reddened. But he inclined his head toward Suker and whispered, "Good to see she hasn't lost her spunk."

Was Razz still sweet on Maggie? My, now there was a thought. Maggie and Razz. Before Suker could explore it, Rob Kelsey walked up, all stormy faced.

"I wanna talk to you, Razz." He included Billy and Martin in his dark look. "You boys too."

"Now what's *that* all about?" Maggie's brow puckered as Rob drew Razz off to one corner. Billy and Martin followed.

Suker shrugged and expanded on her fantasy. Maggie, getting over Rob and marrying Razz instead. What a tie that would be, binding her two families into one. Suker looked from her brother off in the corner with Rob to the stately green cedar to the pretty stained-glass win-

71

dow of the Madonna and Child. She'd heard tell nothing was too hard for God. And today, she reckoned that was so.

The sky was slate gray as they left the church. Suker poked out her tongue and caught her first snowflake of the season. Razz came running to overtake her.

"What'd Rob want?"

"He wanted to know how long I was staying." Razz grinned and strutted along all cocky-like. "I told him about Kitty waiting for me back home, and that settled him down."

What'd that have to do with Billy and Martin? Suker didn't wonder about it long, for the snow, coming down more heavily now, was a distraction.

"Dave says it don't snow often in these parts. But I bet, if we're real good and don't jinx ourselves, we could have a white Christmas," Suker said, and she skipped like a colt, pleasuring in the idea.

Sophie fixed lunch while Dave helped Jeremiah set the table. It was soup again, with a few potatoes floating in it. Whipped eggs gave it color and body. And there were seasoned chunks of dried bread sprinkled on top.

After dishes were washed and put away, Suker brought out her worn deck of cards. She and Razz and Maggie sat in the warm kitchen, teaching Jeremiah how to play pig. Dave scratched numbers in the station's account book while Sophie darned the heels of worn-out socks. Late in the afternoon, Rob Kelsey came to take Maggie out to his folks' house. It was his mother's birthday and they were having a special dinner.

They had fried bread for supper. By the time it was over, there was a three-inch blanket of white on the ground. Kids were out in the snow-lit street playing. Their laughter kissed the windows like frost. Eager to join them, Suker dashed supper dishes through the water.

Jeremiah took the drying towel. He rubbed at every speck she missed. Suker complained, "It'll take forever if you're aiming to rub all the flowers off the plates!"

Dave nudged her aside. "I'll finish, you two. Suker, check-see on Miss Tims. Then you can play in the snow until time for pageant practice."

Ten

With snow and friends tantalizingly close by, Suker went through Miss Tims's chores like a wind over Oklahoma. She pulled on her coat.

"Did you need some coal brought in before I go?"

"No, Susan. I have all I need for now. I'd like a word with you, though." Miss Greer Tims rose from her chair on rail-thin legs. "It concerns your brother and his companions. They're the same two boys I cautioned you about associating with, aren't they?"

"Billy and Martin?" Suker lifted her guard as she nodded.

"Late last night, I saw your brother come down off the tracks. The other two boys were with him. I'd almost bet they'd been kicking coal off a slow-moving freight."

Suker tied her head scarf with a jerk but said nothing.

"I stirred up the fire and made tea, as I was having trouble sleeping," Miss Tims continued. "Next thing I knew, they were in Mr. Tilton's toolshed."

"Must have needed a tool for something."

"Indeed, they did. A saw and an axe, to be specific."

"Dave don't care what they borrow, so long as they put it back."

"Doesn't, Susan. And I'm afraid that's not the point." Miss Tims ignored her impertinent tone. Like a circling vulture staring down her beak, she fixed Suker with a cold, measuring gaze. "I understand a Christmas tree was found at the church this morning. And that no one took credit for it."

Suker's toes curled at the sudden awful prick of anxiety. She licked her chapped lips. "Some folks like to give gifts without taking credit."

"Admirable, I'm sure. Unless their modesty is a cover for thievery."

Her dry words smarted like dust in the eyes. Suker blinked and retorted, "Sophie says it's wicked to gossip about folks. She says it's the same as stealing their good name."

"I am not gossiping, Susan. And you'd do well not to be so insolent."

Suker glared right back at the old stick.

"To continue, just as the boys came out with their tools, that Kelsey fellow brought Margaret home. Your brother and the other two boys threw the tools in the back of the truck and left with Mr. Kelsey."

"Her name ain't Margaret, it's Maggie. And that doesn't prove a thing!"

"Perhaps not. But the truth will come easily enough," said Miss Tims. "The cedar trees that concern me are some my father planted as a border around the cemetery. That was many, many years ago. I would hate to think that a tree which has withstood drought and high winds and pestilence for over a half a century has fallen to tomfoolery."

"Razz wouldn't do that!"

"I'm not at all sure of that. Nor are you." Miss Tims set her narrow shoulders.

"You hate boys! You think they're all no good!" Suker accused, heart pounding.

"I do not bring this matter to your attention to cause you pain, Susan," she said stiffly.

"You're wrong about Razz. He came all this way to see me and he doesn't know a thing about that tree!"

"Then you won't mind going before school tomorrow and asking the sheriff to drive me out to the cemetery, will you?" challenged Miss Tims.

Oh yes, Suker minded. She minded so much, she marched right out, slamming the door behind her. The voices of the neighbor children rang boisterously as they pelted one another with snow. But the storm raging within stole Suker's wish to join them. Miss Tims hated her own brothers and every other male on earth. She spoke out of those mean, bitter feelings. There wasn't a bit of truth to what she was saying.

And yet, as the snowflakes danced before her eyes, Suker couldn't crowd out the absolute knowledge of Razz kicking coal off the train. She'd seen it with her own eyes yesterday. Sophie would say that was stealing. Dave, too. As would Miss Tims. Yet Razz had not viewed it that way. "There's tons of it. They won't miss a bucket or two," he'd said. Could he have taken the tree, feeling no one would miss it either? Hateful doubts crept in and clung like burrs.

What was she to do? Go on defending Razz in blind faith? Or prove to herself that her trust was justified? She'd taken part in enough Christmas tree fellings to know how tree sap turned gloves sticky. But Razz didn't seem to have any gloves. How about wood chips, then? Chips and sawdust such as filled the cuffs of trousers while cutting a tree! Razz was still in the wool trousers he'd worn to church that morning. Which meant the ones he'd worn last night would be in his room. Suker lifted her gaze to the attic window.

Love and loyalty warred with ugly suspicion as she slipped in through the back porch and crept upstairs, a candle lighting her way. The bare plank floor creaked beneath her feet in the still, silent chill of the attic. Eerie shadows flickered about the rafters. Her heart leaped at a small, scurrying sound. Mouse, she reasoned. But the anxious guilt of trespassing kept her heart fluttering as she scanned the floor for wood chips. The candle made such a dim pool of light, it was hard to be sure. But there didn't seem to be any chips or sawdust on the floor.

A mound of blankets and quilts lay rumpled on the narrow cot. There was a comb, soap, and a razor on an upturned orange crate and a folded piece of deer hide containing a hunting knife, matches, a compass, a fishing hook, and some line. She spotted a flour sack half-concealed beneath the bed. It was the one Razz'd been carrying when he arrived yesterday.

Suker pulled it out and held the candle close as she looked inside. Red-flannel underwear and two shirts. Had Sophie collected the trousers to wash? Suker was about to go downstairs and check when she spotted them hanging over a chair back in a shadowy corner. Careful with the candle, she made her way to them.

"So it's you." Razz spoke from the doorway.

Suker spun around, pulse racing.

"I saw the light from the street and wondered who was up here."

"I'm just looking," she blurted, trousers in hand.

"For what?"

"Wood chips." The truth tumbled out. She told him in a rush what Miss Tims had said, then asked point-blank, "Did you put that tree in the church, Razz?"

"Why would I? I didn't even know the church *needed* a tree."

"Billy and Martin knew," she reasoned, giving his trousers a shake.

"So you're saying you believe her?" Defiance crept into his voice.

"She saw you get an axe and a saw from the toolshed. And looky here—wood chips," she added, heart plummeting.

"Sure, it's wood chips. The wind blew a branch across the road down on Billy's street. We had to chop it in two pieces to get it out of the way. You can ask Rob Kelsey. He dropped us off."

Razz blinked and looked her right in the eye. Suker averted her gaze. She remembered racing Razz to the church that morning. *How was it he'd nearly beat her? Had he already known the way?* She thought too of Rob pulling Razz aside.

"What was it Rob Kelsey said to you boys this morning?"

"I told you—he wanted to know how long I was staying. Look, if you don't believe me, then maybe I better climb on the next train and go home!"

Suker heard the hurt in Razz's voice. Chest tight as shrunken cotton, she shivered in the frosty attic. "I believe you. It just upset me, her accusin' you. She's such a nosey old woman."

"Forget her," said Razz. Expression mellowing, he feigned a playful punch at her shoulder. "Now that that's settled, let's go get in on the snow war."

Was it settled? Not altogether. But his denial calmed Suker some. She joined in the shouting and laughing and flinging snow at the neighbor kids, and in no time at all Dave was hollering out the door that it was time for pageant practice. They trooped off through the glittery night, taking Jeremiah with them.

Mrs. Nethers wanted Jeremiah to sing with the angels. But he couldn't be persuaded. Instead, he sat in the front pew watching while Razz horsed around in the back with Billy and Martin. After practice, they took a vote and decided to leave the tumbleweed tree.

"Aren't we going to decorate the big cedar tree?" asked John Paul Ritchie.

"It's beautiful just the way it is," said Mrs. Nethers, smiling.

Suker would have agreed that morning. But it was tainted now, stained by Miss Tims's accusations. She couldn't look at it without getting a jittery stomach.

"It'd be pretty with red ribbons and some glass ornaments," John Paul spoke up again. "Maybe my mama's got some she'd part with."

"He's just being a smarty, 'cause his daddy paid for the tree," whispered the girl next to Suker. "Least, that's what I heard."

Suker caught her breath, praying it was so.

Eleven

The smell of fresh-baked bread and the sound of hushed breakfast voices drifted up from the kitchen. Suker recalled Maggie slipping from between the covers hours ago when the rooster had crowed. Suker was usually an early riser, too. But she felt no zest for this new day. Durn old Miss Tims, anyway. Fetch the sheriff, indeed! Not if she could find a way out.

Feeling twitchy inside, Suker reached for her doll. Nothing but covers. She folded herself over the edge of Maggie's bed and looked beneath it. No Clarisse. Cold floor stinging her feet, she dashed to her own room. Jeremiah was still in bed.

"You got Clarisse again, don't you?" she accused.

His eyelids twitched. He wasn't asleep—only pretending.

Suker scrambled over him and retrieved Clarisse from the far side of the bed. But she swallowed her rebuke, for there were larger matters on her mind. Miss Tims and the sheriff and Razz's character being called into question. She slid Jeremiah a measuring glance. He

81

talked less than any human being she'd ever encountered. A natural-born secret keeper.

"I gotta tell you somethin'," she said, and sure enough, his eyes drifted open. "You know that tree in the church? Miss Tims thinks it came from the cemetery. She thinks Razz and Billy and Martin and Rob cut it down. She wants me to fetch the sheriff to give her a ride out to the cemetery so she can look-see."

"Why?" asked Jeremiah.

"So's she can raise a big stink. If you ask me, it ain't the tree anyway, so much as Miss Tims's dislike of boys," Suker added bitterly.

Jeremiah sucked at a scratched thumb but offered no opinion. The bruise on his face where he'd fallen Saturday had turned a deep purple. That and his missing tooth gave him a defenseless, woebegone look.

She turned toward the door, too many troubles of her own to start feeling sorry for him. Briskly, she said, "We got school. Hurry up, and I'll show you which classroom is yours."

"I'm not going."

"You have to go to school. Besides, if I'm showing you around the school, I won't have time to stop by the sheriff's." She latched on to a perfectly good excuse.

"I'm not going," Jeremiah said again.

He clutched at the sheet, his knuckles white as gravestones. Gravestones! Struck by a sudden idea, Suker let out a yelp. "Why didn't I think of it before? Jere! I'll go to the cemetery and look! That old tree probably didn't even come from there. Get dressed, if yer comin'. The sooner we get there, the sooner I can leave off worryin'."

Jeremiah's lashes came up in a sweep. Something

82

stirred in his brown eyes. "Is the cemetery on the road to California?"

Caught up in her plans, the oddity of the question escaped Suker. She nodded. "Right on Highway 66."

Jeremiah slid out of bed and reached for his trousers.

It was a cold walk, made longer by a wide detour around the Flying Red Horse. But Suker couldn't risk being spotted by Dave or Maggie. Not when they should be in school. Breakfast churned in her stomach as she thought of Razz, still asleep in the attic, no idea she was checking up on him. Suppose there *was* a tree missing. What then?

"You're sure this road goes to California?" Jeremiah interrupted her thoughts.

"Positive." Suker turned and pointed back the way they'd come. "If you follow it far enough in the other direction, it goes clear to Shirley. How 'bout that?"

He glanced back, pain in his gaze, then turned and plodded on. Traffic sloshed past. Some vehicles resembled misshapen packages on wheels, what with ropes strapping everything from dishpans to water cans to crates of poultry to the roofs and bumpers and running boards. Suker might not even have noticed but for the way Jeremiah stared after them.

Suker's fingers had no more feeling than sticks by the time they reached the cemetery. It was bordered by tall trees, just like the Christmas tree in the church. A few feet inside the cemetery, she looked back. Jeremiah had stopped at the gate.

"Aren't you coming?" she asked.

Jeremiah shook his head. He looked like a corn nub,

small and pale and lost in that big, fine coat. She choked down impatience and shrugged. "Wait right here, then."

Suker picked her way between rows of gravestones, moving toward the line of trees Miss Tims'd said her daddy had planted. She was halfway around the cemetery when a gap in the trees became apparent. A knot jerked tight in her stomach. Daylight where greenery should be. Markings in the snow, too. Man-sized footsteps. Several sets. And the feathery smear made by branches where the tree had been dragged. A few yards away, she spotted the raw stump, still oozing sap.

Suker squeezed her fists tight, disappointment bitter tasting. It was just a tree. Not nearly so shameful as a moonshine still. But Razz'd lied. Lied well enough, she'd believed him. A bitter pill, injured trust. She kicked at the nearest gravestone. Pain like liquid fire shot up her leg. It was a distraction. But only for a moment. For when her foot stopped throbbing, her heart set in aching again. She swiped at hot tears with her tattered coat sleeve and started back toward the gate.

A passing truck sloshed wet gray snow on Jeremiah's knickers. He stepped further away from the road and stamped his feet. They tingled like he'd stepped on needles. But his thoughts were on his parents. He'd been thinking about them from the moment he'd awakened. If they'd entered the gate where the angels sang, there was no reason for him to stay in Clement. They weren't going to find the map he'd left and come for him. He'd have to go on to California and be with Bryce.

Trying not to think of dark, dirt-filled holes, Jeremiah gazed across the cemetery in search of Suker. She was coming back. She walked fast, her head down, hands in her pockets.

"Come on," she said without looking at him. "Let's go back."

Jeremiah started after her. It was too cold to walk to California. He would have to ask for a ride, just like Razz had done.

They hiked single file along the shoulder of the highway. Jeremiah made a game of trying to match his feet to Suker's turned-in prints in the snow. They'd almost reached the Flying Red Horse when she stopped short. Jeremiah swung around to stare at the black car that had captured her attention. She moaned.

"That's the sheriff and Miss Tims, headed out to the cemetery! They'll find the stump for sure!"

So her brother *had* stolen the tree. Jeremiah wasn't surprised. Razz'd stolen canned tomatoes, coal from a railway car, and six silver dollars. Why not a tree?

"Suker! What're you doing here?"

It was Maggie, hollering from the door of the station. Reluctantly, Suker went to meet her. Jeremiah stooped down and labored over tying a soggy shoestring. By the time he straightened again, they'd gone inside. He put his nose to the window glass. Suker stood over the coal burner, warming her hands as she and Maggie talked.

"Well, this is a surprise," said Dave, striding toward the station. Jeremiah ducked his head. He heard Dave ask as he went inside, "Suker, why aren't you two in school?"

Jeremiah's heart raced. He had to find a ride to California, fast! The driver of the car Dave'd just filled with gasoline was climbing behind the wheel. Jeremiah rushed over. He swallowed hard and asked, "Are you going to California?"

"Mail route don't go quite that far," the man replied gruffly. "Step back, sonny. I got work to do."

Jeremiah moved toward another car that was sitting off to one side. He explored with his tongue the hole where his tooth had been, and waited for the lady in the car to notice him. She rolled the window down a crack.

"Hallo, little boy. Lost a tooth, did you?"

He nodded. "Are you going to California?"

"Hope to pick peas there," she said.

"May I come too?"

She smiled a weary smile and swept an arm toward the backseat. There was an old woman and raggedy kids too lively to count. "Where would we put you? We're packed in like ticks in a hound dog's ear."

She turned her attention to the sobbing child in her lap. Jeremiah saw a truck with a flat tire limp off the road, then a car. Dave and Maggie filed out of the station. Dave motioned for the truck driver to pull off to one side while Maggie bustled over to the black sedan. Jeremiah followed.

"Can I help you, sir?" Maggie asked the driver.

"Five gallons, and wash the window," said the man, climbing out.

"Yes, sir." Maggie started pumping.

Jeremiah noticed the sharp way the man looked around. His father had been sharp, too, and quick to look about.

A lady got out on the passenger's side. "Don't suppose you've got an indoor toilet?"

"No. But there's a privy out back," said Maggie.

The lady wrinkled her nose as if the arrangement displeased her. She glanced down at Jeremiah in passing. Quickly, he fell in step with her.

"Are you going to California?"

"California? Now there's a grand idea. Yes, I think we shall." She laughed as if the notion pleased her immensely and kept walking.

Jeremiah stared after her as she disappeared into the privy.

"Run along home now, little boy," she said, when she came out and found him waiting.

Jeremiah trailed her to the station but waited outside. He could see Suker through the glass. She was behind the counter. Her eyes were red like she'd been crying. But she was trying to make a sale. "This is real good bread, ma'am. Just ten cents a loaf."

Summoning his courage, Jeremiah started back toward the car. Maggie had finished putting in the gas. Shivering in her light coat, she started back toward the station, calling, "Suker? Could you wash the window while I ring up the sale?"

Jeremiah circled to the other side of the car. The moment Maggie started away, he opened the door, crawled into the back, and curled up, making himself small on the floor.

"Too cold to wash windows," he heard Suker muttering as she sloshed at the glass.

Maggie's startled exclamation carried across the drive. Curious, Jeremiah bolted up in the car. He spotted Maggie inside the station, arms raised like she was reaching for something off a high shelf.

"What's the matter, Mag . . ." Suker's question died on her lips. She blinked as if she couldn't quite believe what she was seeing, then flattened her mouth. "Jeremiah Bishop the Second, what're you doing in there?"

Quickly, Jeremiah ducked down again. She jerked the back door open. "Get out of there! Hurry up before they see you," she hissed.

Jeremiah crowded against the far door. He had to go to California. He wouldn't get out. The car would leave without him.

"Right now!" Suker ordered.

In the same instant, a loud pop rang out. Maggie's scream echoed over the sound of running steps. The man flung himself into the car, gun still in hand.

"Get out, get out, get out!" Suker shrieked.

Jeremiah stumbled in his haste, hit his chin on the bench seat and tasted blood.

Twelve

Suker reached in and jerked Jeremiah out of the car as the engine screamed to life. Limbs entangled, they jumped back from spinning, gravel-spitting tires. The black sedan lurched off the drive and onto Highway 66, gears grinding.

Maggie flew out of the station. "They robbed us! They're getting away!"

Dave came running after her, a shotgun in hand. "You kids get in the station! You too, Maggie!" he ordered as he raced toward the road.

"Are you hurt? Are you shot?" Suker cried.

"I'm fine. Hurry!" Maggie urged them inside.

Suker crowded beside her in the doorway. Breath caught, heart pounding, she looked on as Dave reached the road. He lifted the gun to his shoulder and took aim at the fast-disappearing black sedan. Two cars blipped past, obscuring his view. He lowered the gun and turned back.

"They got away! Low-down, good-for-nothing thieves," Maggie fumed.

"Watch the station, girls," Dave called. "I'm goin' for the sheriff."

"Wait a second! We saw the sheriff headed out toward the cemetery." Suker got her wits about her.

"Isn't that his car coming now?" Maggie pointed.

Sure enough, it was the sheriff. He was headed back toward town, Miss Tims in the passenger's seat. Dave stepped into the road and waved them down. Seconds later, Miss Tims climbed out and Dave climbed in. The sheriff's car whipped around in the road and roared away.

Miss Tims came into the station on her go-to-town cane, eager for details of the robbery. Suker and Maggie took turns telling her what they knew as they waited for Dave and the sheriff to return.

It was an anxious thirty minutes. The bandits had gotten clean away. The sheriff found a bullet imbedded in a Coca-Cola sign just behind the counter where Maggie had stood, ringing up the sale. He pried it out with his knife and held it out for all to see.

"Lucky all they got was five dollars. Could've been your lives."

Gooseflesh chased up Suker's arms. Weak in the knees, she edged closer to Maggie and Dave. "What makes folks go bad like that, anyway?"

"Selfishness," said Miss Tims, though Suker hadn't been talking to her. "It starts small. Like coal snitched from a railway car. Or a stolen cedar tree."

It all came rushing back, then. The tree in the church. The fresh stump in the cemetery. Suker lifted her chin and held her shoulders stiff, not about to let Miss Tims see her worry. But on the inside, she was like a tattered cloth, just barely holding together.

Miss Tims said no more. The sheriff, in a rush to alert neighboring law enforcement authorities to the robbery, didn't mention the cedar tree either. But Suker had an uneasy feeling it was far from a dead issue.

At Dave's request, the sheriff dropped Suker and Jeremiah off at school. Being an eyewitness to a holdup brought a lot of attention her way. Particularly when it got out that she'd pulled Jeremiah from the robbers' car. No one actually called her a hero. But she sure did get treated nice—first at school, then at home.

For once, no one mentioned looking in on Miss Tims. Sophie made depression pudding. Dave read an extra chapter from *A Christmas Carol*. And late that night, when Suker awoke from a dream strewn with cigar-chomping bandits dragging chains like old Marley, Maggie took her downstairs and walked her clear through the house, just to prove there was nobody hiding down there.

But Suker couldn't shake an overshadowing anxiety. She wished she could mention the cedar tree to Razz again. But how could she do so without driving a wedge? And when he'd come so far to see her. The words burned unsaid, and the next day, she came home from school to learn that Miss Tims had filed a formal complaint against Razz, Billy, Martin, and Rob Kelsey.

Maggie, who swore Rob was innocent, was absolutely furious. Sure, he'd given the boys a ride out to the cemetery. But how was he to know they were going to cut down a tree?

The axe and the saw were pretty good evidence, according to the sheriff. Razz never did out-and-out confess. All he would say was that Rob'd been with him and Billy and Martin the night in question. So the sheriff imposed a five-dollar fine upon Rob right along with the others. Five dollars *each* the boys had to pay or serve a week in jail. With Christmas just five days away, it seemed a double tragedy when the sheriff locked them up.

Was Rob guilty, or was Razz making mischief out of jealousy? Suker wondered. She'd seen the way Razz looked at Maggie. And heard him tease, with a special note in his voice.

Innocent or guilty, five dollars was a lot of money. Suker hoped old Miss Tims broke out in blisters. "I'm never again gonna check-see on that old stick. She can just sit over there and rot!"

Sophie pushed her gently into a chair. "I know it seems an overreaction to a boyish prank. But, Suker, you just have to know people the way people are. Don't go getting bitter and hard."

Suker jumped right up again. "Miss Greer Tims is the bitter one and don't ask me to go, 'cause I won't!"

Sophie didn't ask, nor did Dave. Maybe because they saw it was unfair. Or maybe because they were busy sorting it out between themselves how the whole matter should be handled. It didn't help Suker's sense of shame a bit when Martin's mother stopped by the house that evening on her way to pay Martin's fine and take him home.

"What do you mean by opening your home to such a lad in the first place?" she scolded Sophie and Dave. "Bad company sure enough corrupts good morals. Martin's learned it the hard way!" she fumed. Then she fluttered off like a ruffled hen.

Somehow, Billy's folks scratched the money together, too, and set him free. But Rob just plain didn't have it,

92

and neither did his parents. It looked like he and Razz would have to serve out their week term.

Cutting down a tree, Suker knew, was nowhere near as bad as what her daddy had done. Yet shame was shame, and it didn't help any that Razz had lied right to her face. Lied so well that there was a part of her still half believed he'd been unjustly accused.

She went up to her room while it was still early and wrapped herself and Clarisse in a quilt to keep warm. Downstairs, she could hear them talking over the whole situation.

"Reckon if we dig deep enough, we could come close to paying those boys' fines," Dave rumbled.

"Five dollars lost in the holdup, don't forget," said Sophie. "And the gas man comes to fill the tank this week."

"Rob won't let you, anyway. I already offered my bread money. Guess if he wants to be that proud, he'll just have to sit," said Maggie, snippy in her misery.

"Can't very well get one out and not the other," said Dave. "But it sure has put a damper on poor Suker."

"That Razz hasn't learned much in four years. I could wring his dumb woodsie neck!" said Maggie heatedly.

Suker started humming to drown out their voices—humming fiercely and brushing Clarisse's hair. By and by, Jeremiah stole in and stood beside the bed. He'd never said a word about her pulling him out of that car. But ever since, he'd been different toward her. She couldn't say how, exactly, for he hardly talked. Still and all, she didn't object to his company.

By and by, she put Clarisse aside and tried out the thoughts in her head: "I might go see Razz."

Jeremiah just blinked.

"Wanna come?"

He turned away without answering. Suker sighed. He might have changed toward her. But his feelings toward Razz were the same. She pushed back the covers and came to her feet. She'd have to go alone.

It was a dark, cold walk to the jail. The sheriff looked surprised to see Suker. But he unlocked a heavy wooden door and ushered her into a narrow corridor that separated two small cells. Fumes from the lantern burned her nose as she picked out Razz in the furthest of the two. The nearest was empty.

"Where's Rob?"

"You just missed him," said the sheriff, trimming the lantern wick. "Mr. Tucker admitted Rob wasn't party to the tree cuttin', so I let him go."

"Really?" Suker aimed her surprise toward Razz in the far cell.

But it was the sheriff who answered: "That's right. I'll leave you two alone now. Don't be too long, though, Suker. Your folks'll start to worry." He hung the lantern from a hook before leaving.

"Maggie'll be glad about Rob," said Suker, unsure now that she was here what to say or why she'd come.

Behind the steel doors, Razz came off the cot with a shrug. "His folks didn't have the money to free him. What else could I do?"

"Should have told the truth about it in the first place," said Suker, still smarting over his lie.

Misunderstanding, he grinned by the shadowy light. "Won't argue with that. Maggie was here earlier. If not for these bars, she'd have ripped me apart."

She curled her hands around the cold bars. "I *meant*

94

about that tree. Two days ago, you were denying the whole thing."

He shrugged carelessly. "I don't see what you're so mad about. I did it for you."

"Me?" she cried.

"Who else? All you've talked about since I got here was Christmas and how it used to be. I figured a big old tree'd be just the fuss you wanted."

"Well, I sure didn't want it at such a price!" Suker turned away, mad all over again. How could he have changed so much in the years they'd been separated? Or had he changed at all? Had she, in her yearning for him to come, built up a false picture?

Impatient with her thoughts, Suker started home. Dave and Sophie were in the front room. They hadn't even missed her. Rob was there too, sitting next to Maggie. Put out as she was at Razz, it hurt her somehow to see them so happy together. She said good night and slipped upstairs.

But she couldn't calm her thoughts enough to sleep. By and by, Maggie came to bed and drifted right off. Suker tossed and turned and tangled the covers and finally slipped her foot up next to Maggie's. Maggie flinched in her sleep and moved her foot away.

Suker slipped out of bed and past her old room where Jeremiah was sleeping. He had Clarisse again. Somehow, it just didn't matter. She climbed the stairs to the attic room, curled up on Razz's cot, and cried herself to sleep.

Thirteen

———◆———

The next day, on the way home from school, Jeremiah saw the big cedar tree lying in the yard of the lady who didn't like boys. Suker stopped and wagged her head and moped on home to Sophie.

"What's the tree from church doing in Miss Tims's yard?" she asked as Jeremiah trailed her into the kitchen.

Sophie tapped her wooden spoon against the soup pan. "Pastor didn't think it was wise to keep it, under the circumstances."

"*He* put it there?"

"No, he hauled it out to the cemetery. But a couple of mischief-makers brought it back to town and tossed it in Miss Tims's front yard."

Suker flounced into a chair. "What does she need with it? The old stick's got no Christmas in her."

"You're being disrespectful, Suker. Go on upstairs and change out of your school dress." Sophie motioned with her wooden spoon.

Suker bolted out of the chair and clomped up the stairs.

But Jeremiah lingered a moment longer. He asked, "Does the tree belong to her now?"

"I reckon it does," said Sophie.

Jeremiah slipped quietly up the steps.

Suker was stretched out on his bed. It'd been two days since the robbery at the station. She'd been quick when he'd stumbled, trying to get out of the bad man's car. She'd kept him safe. He was glad about that, even if he couldn't go to California.

Earlier, she'd talked about getting a tree for the house. But that was before all the trouble. Maybe she'd forgotten. It worried him, Christmas without a tree. He picked a bit of mud off his shoe and crumbled it between his fingers. "I know where there's a tree."

Suker didn't reply. But when he started away, she got off the bed and put on her coat. The day they'd picked up coal, Jeremiah had noticed the tree. It wasn't green. But it had needles every bit as sharp as the one Sophie used to quilt. He was certain he could find it again, for it was near a tower where the trains stopped to take on water.

It was cold outside. Jeremiah's eyes stung as he led the way up the railroad bank. He tucked his chin to protected his eyes from the bits of cinder and dirt flung by the wind. Suker moped after him, teeth chattering.

"What kind of tree is it?" she asked, when they'd walked a fair distance.

Jeremiah shrugged. He didn't know trees by name. He was glad to see the tower looming on the horizon. "It can't be far," he said.

His toes were numb and Suker was shivering by the

97

time they came to the tree. It was right where he remembered it being.

"Here," he said, pointing.

"It's an old hedge tree. The section man cut it down to keep it from crowding the tracks." Suker rocked back on her heels, looking the tree over.

"It has needles. See?" Jeremiah indicated a prickly cluster.

"Those are thorns." Suker crammed her hands into her coat pockets and cocked her head to one side. "They're kind of like needles, though. I reckon it'd be purty enough, once we hang some decorations."

Jeremiah took hold down near the base where there weren't so many thorns. It was heavier than it looked and hard to drag. But they pulled and puffed and stopped to rest before taking hold again. Bit by bit, they dragged the tree home.

After supper dishes were put away, Jeremiah held the door while Suker hauled the tree in. She hammered boards to the bottom of the tree. Jeremiah's small hands got in the way, and she grazed his thumb once. He winced and popped it into his mouth. But they got the tree to stand without any help from Dave. Together, they gathered the paper decorations from around the house and hung them on the tree.

"You can't come out here yet," Suker hollered to Dave, Sophie, and Maggie. They'd promised to wait in the kitchen until she and Jeremiah finished their "surprise."

Thinking the tree still looked a bit dull, Suker took a mason jar full of old buttons from Sophie's sewing basket. She threaded a thorn right through the holes of a

98

bright gold button, then backed away to admire her handiwork. Pleased, she exclaimed, "Now that adds some sparkle."

Jeremiah reached into the jar and picked out a button. But the holes in the buttons were too small. When he tried to fix it onto a thorn, he pricked his finger.

"You're bleeding. I'll do this part." Suker reached into the jar for a whole handful of buttons.

Jeremiah looked on for a bit, then climbed the stairs and came back down with the treasure sock. He emptied it out onto Dave's chair. Suker caught her breath as earrings and pins and pearls gleamed in the lamplight. She watched Jeremiah pick out a carved cameo and ever so gently, hang it on the tree.

"Oohh, that's purty! And those pearls! Why, they'd be better even than an angel chain!"

Jeremiah hung the pearl necklace, and then a pair of red earrings. Suker's fingers itched to touch the bright baubles. But she held back, trying to be content with watching. By and by, he'd strung every last treasure on the thorny tree.

"That looks just grand, don't it?" sighed Suker.

There was the shine of tears in his eyes as he folded the empty sock into his pocket. His tongue reached for the space where his tooth had been.

"The jewels are the best part, Jere," said Suker, looking away. "Run get Dave and Sophie now."

As the whole family admired the handsome tree, Suker found Christmas had returned to her heart. She even tried to be happy for Maggie over Rob being freed. But that didn't keep her from feeling bad about Razz. It seemed awful harsh, his having to spend Christmas in jail. And all alone, too.

* * *

The next day, Dave paid the fuel man for filling the underground tank. It had been a little less than he'd estimated. That night, Suker overheard him and Sophie talking down in the kitchen. Dave said he had enough left to pay Razz's fine.

But Sophie wasn't in favor of it. "He's gotta learn," she said.

"It's awful hard on Suker," said Dave.

"It's not about Suker. It's about a boy's character. You want to help him or not?"

Suker missed Dave's reply. But Razz's fine went unpaid. She couldn't even be angry at Sophie. Not really. She was just Sophie, doing what she thought was best.

So Suker prayed for five dollars. For a miracle. For Razz to be set free.

But the days were dwindling down. She swallowed her pride and paused on her way up to bed, to plead Razz's case. Edging close to the stove where Sophie was brushing her hair, she balanced on one cold foot and drew the other up beneath the hem of her gown.

"Sophie?"

"Hmmm?"

"I can't see how God'd send Razz all this way just to spend Christmas in jail."

"Wasn't God put him behind bars. It was his own mischief." Sophie reached out and pulled her in. Hugging her close, she whispered, "I'm sorry, Suker, I really am. Don't give you much comfort, I know. But sometimes it's the hard things in life make you strong."

Sophie was right—it wasn't much comfort. Maggie was out with Rob. Suker climbed the stairs and lay in bed all alone, feeling sorry. By and by, Jeremiah crept in.

"Is tomorrow Christmas?" he asked.

"Christmas Eve," said Suker.

"Will there be presents?"

"Nope. Sophie says there'll be no fuss this Christmas."

He slipped beneath the covers. His cold foot grazed her leg. "Mother always wrapped presents," he said, his voice small and lonesome.

"My daddy did, too." Suker sandwiched his foot between hers. She set in telling him how Christmas used to be when she and Razz lived in the woods north of Shirley. She told about cutting their own tree and stringing it with popcorn and cranberries and decorations saved from year to year. She mentioned the good food and the stockings filled with penny candies and fruit. And she told him about Clarisse being her last gift from her father.

Jeremiah hung on to Clarisse. He asked, when she fell silent, "Did you have a party?"

"A Christmas party?" Suker wagged her head.

"My mother liked parties," said Jeremiah. "Do you like parties?"

"Don't know. Never had one," she admitted.

But it sure was something to think about. Suker was still working the idea over when Maggie came home and carried a sleeping Jeremiah off to his own bed.

Easing into it slowly, she said, "How come they don't have a party after the pageant?"

"Are you kidding? No one feels like a party this year." Maggie slipped shivering beneath the covers.

"Why not?"

"It's been a terrible year! Folks from the farms and the shops giving up and moving on. And then all the fuss over that cedar tree. Five dollar fine, in times like these! Folks are mad at Miss Tims and mad at the sheriff and mad at . . . well, just mad for the sake of being mad."

Mad at Razz. That's what she'd started to say. Quickly, Suker countered, "Maybe they need a party to stop being mad."

"A Christmas truce? I don't know, Suker. I don't think it'd work." Maggie yawned and closed her eyes, unaware she'd given Suker just the guidance she needed.

If there was to be a party, it'd have to be a surprise party. Her surprise, and Jeremiah's.

Fourteen

After Saturday lunch, Suker and Jeremiah stole out the back door and went knocking.

In no time at all, they'd invited most everyone to their surprise party. Friends, neighbors, teachers, the postman, the preacher, the choir director, the sheriff. Even Mrs. Webb, who'd been so snippy over Razz's bad company corrupting Martin's good morals. They were almost home when Jeremiah pointed out Miss Tims's house.

"Are you going to ask her?"

Suker shook her head. "She wouldn't come, anyway."

"Why not?"

"She just wouldn't." Remembering what she'd said to Maggie about folks being mad, Suker rubbed her cold hands together and said with a sniff, "Ask her, if you don't believe me."

"She doesn't like boys," Jeremiah reminded. "You ask."

Suker wanted to refuse. But it wouldn't be noble. Not if there was to be a true Christmas truce. She squared her thin shoulders and marched right up to the door. Miss Tims opened it even before she knocked.

"I see you have the boy with you. Perhaps, with his help, you could move that tree." Miss Tims gestured with a boney hand toward the cedar tree on the front lawn. "It'll kill any hope of grass if it's left there till spring."

Suker poked her hands in her pockets. "I didn't come to do chores."

"You've come about your brother, then." Miss Tims clutched her black shawl and waggled one finger. "He has a flaw, you know. A blemish in his character."

"I don't want to talk about that, either."

Miss Tims's mouth bunched up. "What is it, then?"

"You're invited to a Christmas party. It'll be at our house after the pageant."

Recovering from her surprise, Miss Tims pinched her mouth up like a prune. "Are your parents aware you've invited me?"

"The whole town's comin'," Suker sidestepped her question.

"As you know, I'm not one for attending parties. I might take in the pageant, though. What time does it begin?"

"Six-thirty."

"Six-thirty," Miss Tims echoed. "Now about that tree—when will you be able to move it?"

Suker turned and bolted away like a cold, bucking truck.

"Susan!"

Suker kept walking. Jeremiah hazarded a nervous glance back. "She's talking to you," he whispered.

From her own front yard, Suker turned and hollered,

104

"I'm not moving that tree, Miss Tims. Not so long as my brother's in jail. And you can't make me!"

So much for the Christmas truce. Suker kicked at a tumbleweed and sped on across the yard.

After supper, Sophie rushed the whole family through the dishes, through washing and brushing and changing into Sunday clothes and getting out the front door. Just ahead of them, bathed in the light of the streetlamp, Miss Greer Tims was tap-tap-tapping along the walk with her go-to-town cane.

"My soul, I do believe she's going to church!" murmured Sophie in wonder. She glanced at Suker. "This walk is treacherous underfoot. Go on up there and offer her your arm."

Suker hunched inside her coat. "Do I have to?"

"Suker!" Sophie admonished.

"That's all right. I'll do it," Maggie said quickly.

Suker scuffed along, grumbling justifications inside her head. Jeremiah matched his steps with hers, and it wasn't long before they swept right past Maggie and Miss Tims.

Freed to think ahead, Suker warned, "Sophie always dawdles after services. But tonight, we've got to get home fast for the party." They rounded the corner and started up Church Street. "You be waiting at the back door soon as the pageant's over, hear?"

Jeremiah nodded. Just ahead, lamplight shone friendly through the windows of the church. Suker hurried in from the cold night, with Jeremiah at her heels. She saw, as they hung up their coats, that the tumbleweed tree had been moved to the back. Its humble artistry gave the dark vestibule a soft slash of color.

Up front, a plank stable spilled dusty straw everywhere. It took up nearly all the raised platform. There was a door beside it. On the door was a crudely lettered sign which read INN. Suker greeted her friends and Mrs. Nethers and took her place behind the door. She watched through a wide crack as the latecomers filed in. All around her hummed a low-pitched excitement. The choir director whispered last minute instructions to the children, then sat down in the front row.

Suker spotted Dave, Sophie, and Jeremiah along the inside aisle near the front. Folks scrunched together to make room for more. Full as the church was, it would have held Razz. He'd come so far—seven hundred-odd miles! Suker's heart felt punctured, just thinking of him.

The pianist began playing "Silent Night," and the whispers ceased. Down the center aisle came angels singing. Little baby angels, stumbling over their feedsack gowns. Taller angels with glittery halos, helping the babies along. Singing. All singing.

John Paul Ritchie rose from his seat beside Mrs. Nethers. He started reading the Christmas story. Joseph and Mary came slowly up the aisle. Yellow-haired Mary's face glowed with the honor of acting out the most coveted role. She laid her hand on Joseph's arm. He helped her up the steps. They stopped right in front of Suker's door. Nerves tingled along her spine. She caught her breath, awaiting her moment.

The music stopped. The candlelit stage was a holy place with all those angels and all that hush. Joseph drew forward another step. He knocked loud and bold.

The door didn't really open. Suker stepped out from behind it. She put on a cold face and waved her arm, all lofty and superior.

"No room," her voice rang out over the whole church.

Mary dropped her golden head as Joseph persisted. "But we've traveled so far!"

Suker looked out over the audience. It was an awesome thing, all those eyes upon her. One pair stood out from the rest. Fawn eyes, riveted to the scene. Pleased with her captive audience, she bellowed once more, "No room!"

"But we've looked everywhere," cried Joseph.

Beyond him, a short, pudgy form in a fine wool jacket and knickers slipped into the aisle. Jeremiah! Suker's heart bumped as he outdistanced Sophie's reaching arm.

"There's not a room in the while city," Joseph continued. "And my wife's so tired!"

He kept coming. Climbing the steps!

"Please, couldn't you just let her rest for a while?"

Distracted, Suker's wild glance flew back to Joseph. Had he finished his lines? Flushing at the awkward silence, she thundered once more, "No room!"

The angels sang softly. Joseph gave Mary his arm. She hung her shining head, sad as if heaven itself had refused them. Together, they turned away. And there was Jeremiah, eyes shimmering with tears. He reached out as if to touch Mary.

"Wait," he said, his bottom lip quivering. "Wait!"

A tingling silence fell over the church. Unaware he held every beating heart in his hand, Jeremiah whispered, "Please don't go. There's room. Tell them, Suker. Tell them there's room."

Suker caught her breath in that unnatural quiet, knowing that history had written the script. But there was Jeremiah, pleading with his whole being. Begging as if life

107

itself hung in the balance. A sadness swept over her, like the sorrow of separation. She thought, in that heartbeat, of Razz, alone in jail. Of Miss Tims, cut off by old wounds and stiff-necked pride. Of folks fleeing Oklahoma, because there was no room any longer for their way of life.

Was there no end to being no room?

Suker lifted her face and met Joseph's wide gaze. She stretched out a hand and beckoned, saying, "Come back, you two. You can have my room."

Fifteen

———◆———

The shepherds called on the newborn king at the inn instead of in the stable. The wise men and the angel choir, too. They said their lines and sang their anthems. As the last song faded, the audience broke out in a thunderous applause.

Suker flew down a side aisle even before the clapping stopped. Jeremiah was waiting at the door. Waiting like she was someone he could depend upon. Someone he could trust. She plowed into her coat and followed him out, heart swelling with good feelings.

Just ahead of them on the walk was Miss Tims. Suker hesitated only a moment before hurrying to overtake her. "Sure you don't want to come to the party?"

"I have an appointment downtown," she said in that stiff way of hers.

"But it's Christmas Eve. Everything's closed."

"Run along home, Susan. A good hostess doesn't keep her guests waiting." Miss Tims turned with a tap of her cane and headed toward the business district.

Suker scratched her head and watched the darkness

swallow up the old woman. Couldn't be going out to curse her dead brothers. The cemetery was in the other direction. Maybe the ghost of Christmas past was leading her along.

Shivering, Suker nudged Jeremiah into motion. "We better hurry."

Jeremiah raced home beside her. He fetched coal for the kitchen while she hunkered down in the front room, making a fire in the wood stove. Maggie burst in on Rob's arm, big eyed and a-flutter.

"How many, Suker? Just how many did you invite?"

Suker adjusted the draft and blinked the smoke from her eyes. "How many folks live in Clement?"

Maggie's hand flew to her cheeks. "What're we going to feed them? Had you thought of that?"

Suker traded glances with Jeremiah who'd just come in with his hands all blackened by coal. He lifted his shoulders as if to say it hadn't occurred to him either.

Maggie fluttered off to the kitchen. "Come help me, Suker. We can surely find something."

The front room opened and Sophie sailed in.

"Quick, before Mama comes home and her heart flat gives out," added Maggie, unawares.

"Calm down, Maggie. My heart's just fine." Sophie peeled off her coat and passed it to Rob. She beckoned, saying, "I'd thank you to be in charge of coats, Rob. Pile them upstairs on our bed."

Maggie came flying back through the dining room. "Mama, they've invited the whole town!"

"First things first." Sophie stooped down and gathered Suker and Jeremiah in her arms. The scent of face powder, lilac water, and the cold outdoors was all mixed up in her hug. "I've seen a lot of pageants in my life,

110

but that was the best yet. You brought Christmas the way it ought to have been. Made me ashamed to think I'd said there'd be no fuss."

Suker's heart swelled as Sophie planted kisses, one apiece. "Now about this party—"

"Everyone, Mama! Everyone in Clement!" said Maggie as if Sophie hadn't caught it the first time.

"We'll make do." Sophie released them. She smoothed down her dress and patted her eyes dry. "There's popcorn down in the cellar. Jere, run get it. Wash your hands, first. Suker, bring the lantern from the lampstand upstairs. Maggie, run down the street and tell Mr. Markham to bring his fiddle. Dave can dust off his mouth organ and we'll have some music."

"Where *is* Dave?" asked Suker, already in motion.

"He'll be along shortly. Run on upstairs now. We're going to light up this house."

Folks started arriving within minutes. Sophie greeted them just as calm as if she'd had days of preparation. Happy Markham came with his fiddle, and Mr. Blossom brought his guitar. Happy took time from tuning his instrument to nudge Suker with his bow.

"Jest what kinda crazy stunt was that you pulled? No more lines than that, couldn't you have got 'em straight?"

A slow burn crept up Suker's collar. But she mashed her lips together and turned away from butting heads with the grumpy old mail carrier. Off in the kitchen popping popcorn with Maggie, Mrs. Nethers said in a voice that carried clear as a bell, "It was unconventional but a fine presentation overall."

"I liked it." Round, jolly Mr. Blossom winked at Suker and hit an opening chord on his guitar.

Folks seemed evenly divided on the subject. Her daddy used to say opinions were like belly buttons— everybody had one. Course nobody went around airing *them*. Opinions should be so private, thought Suker, sensitive to the harsh ones.

The music was a welcome diversion. The young folks moved the dining room table into the front room and started in dancing. Other folks, some with toddlers underfoot, drifted toward the front room. A card game commenced among the men. The ladies gathered around the quilting frame. Sophie was quick to supply needles. They stitched and visited and warned the little ones away from the thorn tree.

Several girls had brought their dolls along. They built houses with sticks from the kindling basket and played a game called Eviction. Jeremiah watched a moment, then went off to the kitchen where older youngsters had gathered, some to play checkers on a hand-painted board, some to play card games.

It was, to Suker, a thing of pride, the way it came together. The music, the laughter, the racing and chasing of kids feeding off one another's excitement. It was a fine party. A fuss beyond anything she had imagined. Razz was all that was missing.

Separation was a hard thing, especially at Christmas. But what was to keep her from going to him? She wouldn't have to stay long. No one would even miss her. Suker picked a path through the dancers on her way to the back door. She sidestepped a whole circle of kids playing pounce, a noisy game of dried peas, wooden pegs, and a crashing pan lid.

"Do you want to play, Suker?" Billy Brisco invited.

Before Suker could answer, Dave strode in through

the laundry porch. Sophie came into the kitchen at the very same moment. She looked past him, then back again. "I thought you were gettin' him."

Suker split a glance between them. "Gettin' who?"

Sophie's brow furrowed. "What happened?"

Dave wagged his head. "Miss Tims was there."

"Razz? You mean Razz? You were gonna get him out?" cried Suker, hopes freshening.

The noise of the pounce game suddenly quieted. All eyes turned to Dave. He peeled off his coat and his hat and passed them to Suker. "I tried, Suker. But Miss Tims wouldn't hear of it. She said if it had to be done, then—"

He paused. A slow grin spread across his face as he reached behind him and pushed the door open. "Merry Christmas, Suker, from Miss Tims."

There in the doorway stood Razz. Hugging him, dancing foot to foot, Suker cried, "She paid your way? She really truly bought you out?"

"Not exactly." Razz roughhoused out of her hug. "According to her, someone had to pay. So she talked the sheriff into letting her serve the next few hours in my place. I got to be back by midnight."

"Now isn't that jest like her!" exclaimed Suker.

"Before you say anything mean, you should know she called you a lily." Razz wagged his head, his laughter fading to a puzzled grin. "She's an odd one, isn't she?"

"She's talking about my name. Means 'lily,' that's what she's saying."

"I know. But she says it fits you, Suker. And that we ought not to waste such a name as that. Who'd think of such a thing?"

"Miss Tims." Suker flushed and ducked her head and

113

wondered deep inside if maybe she ought not start answering to that name. The one her mother gave her.

Razz went back to the jail at midnight and served out his time. He stayed another five days in Clement. He spent the last one sawing up the tree on Miss Tims's lawn and stacking it for stove wood near her back door. Then he packed up his meager belongings.

Suker walked him to the Flying Red Horse, where he planned to catch a ride east. It was an hour before a trucker came along and agreed to take Razz as far as Springfield, Missouri.

"What're you gonna do, back in Shirley?" Suker asked as the trucker went inside to pay.

"Look after my trap lines. Hunt and fish and when spring comes, maybe I can find farm work." Razz tossed his white sack into the seat and rubbed her head.

Heart aching already, she dug a toe in the Oklahoma dust and ventured, "You'll come again, won't you, Razz?"

"Sure. It's not so far, really. You keep your head up now, and don't let folks beat you down, you hear?"

"I hear."

He grinned his foxy grin and climbed up in the cab to wait for the driver. But instead of closing the door, he reached out and dropped six silver dollars in her hand. "This belongs to Jere."

Suker caught a sharp breath, her hand closing on them. Jeremiah'd been right. He'd been right all along! Shame blew over her like a fiery wind, too hot even for words.

"It's not what you're thinking," said Razz, watching

her face. "California's a long way, and Bryce was short on cash."

Suker darted him a wary glance. "You sayin' Bryce was going to take Jeremiah's money? But how did you know?"

"Saw him meddling with the kid's treasure sock. Course he made an excuse when he saw me looking and quick-like, shoved the sock back under the seat. First chance I got, I took Jere's money for safekeeping. Wasn't long after that, Bryce put me out of the car."

Careful lest the big boulder lift off her chest only to drop again, Suker reasoned, "You should have given it back to him once you got here. Or were you afraid he'd get the wrong idea, and think you stole it?"

"That thought came to mind," Razz admitted. "And I sure didn't want such a rumor reaching Maggie's ears."

So he *was* still sweet on Maggie!

"I figured I'd put it in his suitcase once we got to the house and let him think he'd just misplaced it," Razz was saying, as the trucker circled the truck, checking his tires. "But you pretty much ruined that by saying you'd been all through his suitcase and his money wasn't there."

Heat crept up Suker's collar as she realized how she'd complicated things. Her fingers closed around the coins. "You kept it safe, that's what counts. Wait'll I tell Jere he was wrong about you."

Razz wagged his head. "You can't, Suker. Bryce Bishop isn't much, but he's all the family Jere's got."

"But if I don't tell him the truth, he'll go on thinking poorly of you!"

Razz shrugged as if it didn't matter.

"But what about Maggie?" she protested. "What's she gonna think?"

He grinned carelessly. "After that tree episode, I got no reputation with Maggie, anyway."

It saddened Suker, his giving up on Maggie, and giving up his reputation, too. It just didn't seem fair. But at his insistence, she gave her word she wouldn't tell Jere that *Bryce* was the scoundrel, not Razz.

The driver crawled behind the wheel and let off the brake. The truck started rolling. She moved alongside, waving and holding back tears.

Razz lowered his window and called, " 'Bye, Suker. You keep writin'. And quit your snifflin'. I'll get out this way again."

He said it so easily. A promise he might or might not keep. That was Razz. The truck faded fast as it carried him away, but the memories were sharp and clear. Suker licked her cracked lips and let the hurt of good-bye blow clean. Head up, she started home along Highway 66, pleasuring in knowing where it went. And just how far she'd come.

WORLDS OF WONDER
FROM
AVON CAMELOT

THE INDIAN IN THE CUPBOARD
Lynne Reid Banks   60012-9/$3.99US/$4.99Can

THE RETURN OF THE INDIAN
Lynne Reid Banks   70284-3/$3.50US only

THE SECRET OF THE INDIAN
Lynne Reid Banks   71040-4/$3.99US only

BEHIND THE ATTIC WALL
Sylvia Cassedy   69843-9/$3.99US/$4.99Can

ALWAYS AND FOREVER FRIENDS
C.S. Adler   70687-3/$3.50US/$4.25Can